Lodge Sinister

Lodge Sinister

Dana Ross

THORNDIKE
CHIVERS

This Large Print edition is published by Thorndike Press®, Waterville, Maine USA and by BBC Audiobooks, Ltd, Bath, England.

Published in 2004 in the U.S. by arrangement with Maureen Moran Agency.

Published in 2004 in the U.K. by arrangement with the author.

U.S. Hardcover 0-7862-6552-3 (Romance)
U.K. Hardcover 0-7540-6999-0 (Chivers Large Print)

The text of this Large Print edition is unabridged. Other aspects of the book may vary from the original edition.

Set in 16 pt. Plantin by Elena Picard.

Printed in the United States on permanent paper.

British Library Cataloguing-in-Publication Data available

Library of Congress Cataloging-in-Publication Data

Ross, Dana, 1912–
    Lodge sinister / by Dana Ross.
        p. cm.
    ISBN 0-7862-6552-3 (lg. print : hc : alk. paper)
    1. Married women — Fiction. 2. Lumber trade — Fiction. 3. Large type books. I. Title.
PR9199.3.R5996L63 2004
    813′.54—dc22   2004045982

To my good friend Dr. Len Morgan and his charming wife, Avis, who doesn't have to try to do better.

Chapter One

From the start there had been that haunted look in the pale-blue eyes of Charles Prentiss. Although he had been brought to the Portland Hospital as a badly injured patient, there had been something about him beyond his physical injuries. He had the air of someone still shocked from some macabre experience. Someone who had gone far beyond the edge of ordinary existence to encounter an overwhelming ordeal of a terrifying nature that he could not forget!

Lucy Stanley had come to him as his private nurse late one afternoon on a typical, wintry, January day. She was used to the bitter Maine weather, as she'd grown up in Portland, and had returned there only a few months earlier following the death of her husband. His death had occurred more than a year ago, but it had taken her some time to sell the pleasant home in the South Carolina town where they had been living and settle the balance of her affairs there.

As soon as she'd been free she'd automatically come north. While she had no immediate family living in Portland, there were cousins and aunts and uncles there. Her own mother had married again and was living in Florida, and her father was dead many years. Since she was an only child, this left her very much alone. It had seemed the sensible thing for a healthy, twenty-five-year-old widow without children to find a job. And so she had returned to her profession of nursing.

She'd decided to take on private-duty cases for a start as this gave her a choice of how much she would work. She'd located a small apartment and was gradually building a modest social life. Once again she'd found a niche for herself and was looking forward to a quiet, pleasant existence. Then she'd taken on the case of Charles Prentiss.

Miss Wood of the agency had phoned her in an exultant mood to say, "I've a wonderful case for you to go on!"

Even in her short experience of working for the agency Lucy had learned to be suspicious of Miss Wood's enthusiasms. The elderly spinster had a sly way of passing off difficult cases as pleasant challenges. Lucy feared this might be just another such instance.

So she said cautiously, "What sort of case?"

"An accident victim. His name is Charles Prentiss. One of the Prentiss lumber barons. Surely you've heard of them?"

"I've been away so long I'm out of touch with the local families," she said.

"But you grew up here! You should have heard of the Prentiss lumber companies. But I suppose you mightn't have. They are located far up North. In fact their principal mill town is located close to the Canadian border. It's only a mile or so until you're in Quebec."

Lucy listened to this long harangue with increasing suspicion. She said, "What sort of accident did he have?"

"He was caught in a conveyor belt in one of the mills," Miss Wood explained. "He came into the hospital a few days ago, and they thought they might have to amputate his left leg — but they saved it and he's doing well."

"I see. Just a leg injury."

"He was cut and bruised in many places, but they are only minor," Miss Wood said. "His leg is the main thing. He wants nurses around the clock and he can afford them. The girl I had on the four-to-midnight shift has a sick baby at home and had to give up the case. I have old Mrs. Russell on for days and Miss Blaine for nights. If I can get you on the in-between shift I'll have it all settled."

"I'd prefer a day case," she said.

"I know," Miss Wood agreed. "But you'll find this easy and pleasant. He's very nice. Not an old man. He's in his late thirties, a widower with an invalid son of seventeen. Good-looking with golden-brown hair and interesting blue eyes. He's had a tragic life for a young man of such wealth!"

Lucy said, "I don't need a complete description of him, Miss Wood."

"Well, I thought you ought to know something about him," the spinster head of the agency said. "He's not really old and he's had such bad luck."

"All right," she said. "I'll take the case. I'd say just having the sort of accident he had would be bad enough luck for anyone."

"That's only part of it," Miss Wood said sadly. "His wife was killed in an accident and his son crippled in a shooting accident — and a wheelchair case for life! And that at only seventeen!"

"Ill luck does seem to hound the family," she agreed.

"There is no question of that," Miss

Wood had said at the other end of the line. "Then I'll count on you coming in at four."

"I'll be there," she promised.

Later she was to wonder what her life might have been like if she'd not made that promise. For taking on the care of Charles Prentiss was destined to be a turning point in her affairs. But she had no idea of that when she reported for duty in her smart white uniform and cap that same afternoon.

Old Mrs. Russell of the nearsighted, peering eyes behind heavy, horn-rimmed spectacles met her in the corridor a short distance from the private room. The old nurse halted and leaned toward her in a confidential manner.

"So you're the replacement for the next shift?" she said.

"Yes," Lucy said with a faint smile. "I hear the patient is an easy one to look after."

"Very good," Mrs. Russell said, peering at her anxiously. "But he's in a good deal of pain, especially when he moves. And there is something about him."

Her eyebrows lifted. "Something about him?"

"I don't know how to explain it," Mrs. Russell worried. "But there are times he doesn't talk and just sort of stares. You'd think he was seeing some sort of ghost over your shoulder."

"Oh?"

The old woman nodded. "I suppose I'm making too much of it, but he acts as if he had some dreadful secret he's keeping to himself."

"It could be the shock of the accident," she suggested.

"That is true," old Mrs. Russell agreed. "He stumbled on a platform and a second later he was caught in the conveyor belt. If his younger brother hadn't been close by and saved him, I expect he would have been killed."

"I can well believe that," she said. "Lumber mill machinery is always so open. It has to be dangerous."

"I had a cousin worked in a lumber mill," Mrs. Russell said. "I always worried about him being crippled, but he never was."

"I suppose like everything else it is a matter of chance," she said.

The old woman nodded. "Yes. I guess that's it. You can never predict anything. But you needn't worry, this is an easy case."

She left the old woman and went on to

the private room. She had the usual feeling of tension she always experienced when taking on a case. But there was nothing in her brisk manner to suggest this nor was there any expression of uneasiness on her pretty, even-featured face. When she entered the room the man in bed was propped up on pillows and his eyes were closed.

He opened them as she approached his bed. He was a thin man and he would undoubtedly be tall. His face was strong, with high cheekbones and pale, haunted blue eyes. He managed a faint smile as he spoke to her, saying, "You're my new nurse, I assume."

She returned his smile. "You assume right. My name is Stanley, Lucy Stanley."

"I'm Charles Prentiss," he said, holding out a powerful hand for her to shake. "And I can't forgive myself for allowing myself to wind up in a predicament like this."

"It happens to a lot of people."

"So I've been told," he said wryly. "But it doesn't make it any easier for me to accept."

"I understand you are making great progress," she said. "And that is the main thing."

He raised his eyes to the ceiling in a ges-

13

ture of woeful resignation. "Making progress isn't enough," he said. "This is the middle of our busy season! Know anything about the lumber business?"

"Not a thing," she admitted.

"Well, my brother and I are deep in it, a long-time thing, you know. A family business handed down to us. We operate along the Canadian border and our main town is Seven Timbers. Ever hear of it?"

"I'll have to say no."

The handsome man in the bed showed surprise. "Well, it's a big town in the lumber business. Most of the Prentiss operations are located there. Named after seven timbers on a high hill above the town. They sort of stood out, I guess. Gone long ago, but the town still has that name."

"Interesting."

He seemed pleased. "You think so? I'm glad. I like to talk about Seven Timbers and what we do there. Small town. Roads are so bad several months out of the year you can only get in and out easily by plane or the railway. We have a train come through twice a day. We're lucky enough to be on an important freight line, and they carry one passenger car."

She said, "It sounds isolated."

14

"It is," he assured her. "But it's great lumber country. The town is no more than a village. We have about a hundred families, and most of them work for us. We own the stores, hire a company doctor, and help keep the school up to standard." He paused and smiled. "I guess you could call it a company town."

"I lived in the South," she said. "We have some down there. But they are mostly cotton mill towns."

Charles Prentiss showed interest. "You have no Southern accent."

"No," she said. "I was beginning to pick one up. I'd been there three years when my husband died."

"I'm sorry. It must have been sudden. I mean, he would have to be young."

"Yes," she said with a sad little smile. "He was. He had a brain tumor. It happened quickly. A few months and it was over."

"They couldn't do anything?"

"No. It was inoperable. We had the best advice."

The handsome face of the man in the bed shadowed. "That's too bad. Any children?"

"I'm afraid not."

"Left you alone."

"Yes. That's why I'm back here and nursing."

Charles Prentiss frowned. "Life can be a cruel business. I lost my wife a couple of years ago. Tragic accident. She fell down a steep stairway, and we didn't find her until some time later. The fall killed her."

"Were you able to get her to a hospital?"

"No use," he said. "The doctor pronounced her dead as soon as he examined her. If she'd lived we'd have put her on a plane and brought her here in a half-hour or so, just as they did with me."

"I see," she said.

"As long as the weather is all right we have no problem getting people to a hospital quickly," he explained. "Now, if there's a storm, that is another matter. Part of the problem of living in a tiny village."

"I can understand that," she said.

He smiled ruefully. "I'm rambling on too much. You have your work to do. I'm sorry."

"It's all right," she said. And she picked up his chart from the foot of the bed to check it. She noted the various entries and the medication he was supposed to have. In every respect he had lived up to his reputation of being interesting and pleasant. He had the assured air of someone who al-

16

ways had known wealth, and his speech was that of a person of some culture. She could picture him as an Ivy League college man who had entered the family lumber business because it was the thing to do.

Not too much more was said that night. The doctor came for an early-evening visit, and afterward she gave Charles Prentiss the fairly heavy medication that had been ordered for him. This put him to sleep almost at once. She remained in the room reading as midnight and her hour of leaving approached. Every so often she glanced at the bed to make sure her patient was sleeping and all right.

Shortly after eleven he began to talk in his sedated sleep. This was unusual in itself. She put down her book and went to stand by his bed with a concerned look on her pretty face. His words had a tormented ring about them, and yet she could not make them out. At least she wasn't able to make proper sentences out of them.

She heard the words "stairs" and "David" repeated over and over again. And then he called out "Sheila" in an almost panicky tone. His shoulders writhed on the pillow and his head twisted from side to side as if he were in torment. She was about to waken him when he suddenly subsided and drifted into a peaceful sleep. She was relieved but still somewhat worried.

Miss Blaine arrived promptly at twelve to take on the night shift. She was elderly, although younger than Mrs. Russell, a tall, bony woman with a horse face decorated with a wart at the left corner of her mouth. She had an unfortunate nervous habit of almost constantly chewing, which drew attention to the wart.

In the corridor Lucy told her, "I think he's all right. But I should mention he had a strange spell of talking in his sleep."

The horse-faced Miss Blaine eyed her scornfully from behind hornrimmed glasses. "That's nothing new," she observed.

"No?" She was surprised.

"No," the older nurse said, chewing as she finished speaking. "He does it every night. Sometimes worse than others."

Lucy said, "Have you told the doctor?"

"I didn't think it worthwhile. Lots of people talk in their sleep."

"Not when they are heavily sedated."

"I've seen patients who were sedated talk plenty," the angular Miss Blaine said, chewing scornfully.

"I know," she said. "But it isn't always a good sign. I think it should be mentioned to his doctor."

"You do it," Miss Blaine challenged her.

"I will," she said. "And you note if he does much of it through the night."

"All right," Miss Blaine said, but she did not sound too interested.

Lucy changed into her street clothes and went downstairs to take a taxi home. It was a blustery, winter's night, and she quickly entered one of the taxis waiting by the hospital entrance and gave the driver the address of her apartment. Then she sat back in the near-darkness of the taxi's back seat to think and relax.

She was wearing a pert muskrat turban perched on her short-cut black hair. She held her fur-trimmed cloth coat tightly about her, as the taxi was not all that warm. Her oval face and her large green eyes held a slightly puzzled expression as she thought about Charles Prentiss. She had taken an instant liking to the handsome man, but at the same time she was mystified by him. There was that strangeness in his manner that suggested a dark secret closely held. She felt it could be put down to the tragic death of his wife and the crippling accident that had overtaken his only son. These things would be enough to upset almost anyone — and especially a man as sensitive as the youngish lumber baron.

19

His rantings while under sedation also had caught her attention. He had mentioned the names of his son and late wife, among other things, and this suggested that he was still deeply bothered by what had happened. His description of the mill town had been typical. She was sure that she'd seen many such places — bleak and isolated, and dominated by one industry. It meant the Prentiss family and any other of the rich owners in the town must possess great wealth.

And great power! She glanced out the car window into the dark streets of the winter night. And she wondered why she found herself so deeply concerned about this man she'd barely met. She was to ask herself this question many times again.

That night her sleep was interrupted by a series of strange dreams in which the handsome lumber baron played a role. She dreamed of being there by the long conveyor in the mill when he'd toppled down into it. She heard his frantic scream as he fell and the shouts of horror as the machinery was stopped. And then she saw a forbidding female figure standing back in the shadows at the scene of the accident with her face hidden by a scarf she wore to shield her head. Lucy awoke from this dream trembling and drenched with per-spiration!

She felt that she was behaving in a ridic-ulous fashion and tried to put the weird dream out of her mind and get back to sleep. But the dream haunted her! She lay there staring up into the shadows for a long while, thinking about it and what it might mean.

The next day when she reported for work she inquired when his doctor might be expected on the floor. And when she learned that the surgeon was still at the head nurse's desk, she went to talk with him before going to the private room of Charles Prentiss.

The surgeon, a mild-mannered, aging man, listened to her with interest. When she'd finished, he said, "I'm glad you've told me this. I would have expected the se-dation to take care of any unpleasant nightmares on the patient's part, but evi-dently it hasn't."

"I felt I should mention it," she said.

"And you are right," he agreed. "I'll talk to the patient later and probably change the medication. It would seem that in addi-tion to his injury he is suffering from some sort of emotional strain of which I haven't been aware."

"That could be," Lucy agreed. Indeed, she felt this was only too likely to be the case.

The doctor studied her with interest. "You are Mrs. Stanley, the new nurse," he said.

"Yes," she said, somewhat embarrassed.

"I wonder if this has been going on since he came to the hospital?"

"I think so," she said. "Miss Blaine, the night nurse, told me it was nothing new."

The surgeon frowned slightly. "And yet she didn't mention it to me. Well, I must thank you for your competence. I'll look into this."

She left him and went on to the room occupied by Charles Prentiss. When she entered it she found a man standing by his bedside who so greatly resembled the handsome, brown-haired man that there could be no mistaking it was his brother. This younger man had lighter brown hair and his features were a little coarser than those of his brother.

Charles smiled at her from the bed and said, "Here she is!" And he introduced her to his brother.

Ned Prentiss shook hands with her and gave her a shrewd appraisal with his keen blue eyes. He said, "You must have impressed Charles. He has talked more about you than any of his other nurses."

She laughed. "That's because I'm still a novelty. I only came with him yesterday."

Ned said, "You must have special powers. I think my brother shows more progress in the last twenty-four hours than I've noticed since he came in here."

"The doctor promises me I'll be walking with a cane and be able to leave here in a month," Charles said.

"Great," was his brother's comment. "That will get you back to us for mid-February. We need you!"

Charles turned to her and said, "You left while I was asleep last night."

"Yes," she said, a little embarrassed by the memory of his nightmares.

"I was disappointed when I awoke and found you gone," he told her. "Miss Blaine isn't exactly a comforting type. But then I don't have much to do with her, since I'm asleep most of the time she's here."

Ned spoke up, "I'll leave you, Charles, now that Mrs. Stanley is here. I have a few business matters to look after."

"But you'll be back?" his brother said.

"Yes," the younger man replied. "I'll come back and have a light snack here at the hospital. Mabel is meeting me here.

Then we will go to the airport and fly back home." He turned to her. "Mabel is my wife. I'll want you to meet her."

"Thank you," she said.

Ned sighed. "Well, no point in lingering. I'll see you both later." And with a cheerful nod for them he went on his way.

After he'd left the room, a weary shadow crossed the face of the handsome man in bed. "I feel like a criminal," he said. "Leaving everything on Ned's shoulders at our busiest season."

"You worry too much!" she chided him. "You should concentrate on recovering. It's not your fault you had the accident."

"It was clumsy of me," Charles Prentiss said grimly. "I still can't understand how I happened to lose my balance. One moment I was standing there gazing over at the conveyor and in the next instant I was falling through the air down onto it. To make it worse, Mabel had come down to the mill on one of her infrequent visits and was there on the platform with me when it happened. I can still hear her screams!"

A chill ran along Lucy's spine as she thought of her eerie dream of the night before in which she'd had a vision of the accident. There had been a woman lurking in the shadows in the dream fantasy. And she'd not even known that this Mabel had been standing there! Did it have some meaning?

She tried not to show her feelings and very casually said, "Most accidents are like that. In reviewing them it's difficult to explain how they came about."

"I suppose so," Charles Prentiss said with a sigh. "Anyway, I'm here! And you're right. The important thing is to recover and get back home."

She said, "You and your brother are the sole managers of your lumber business?"

"Along with my brother-in-law, John Rhode," Charles Prentiss said. "He has a share in the mill. So he has continued on with us even after my wife's death. There are a half-dozen families own all the businesses in the area. My wife, Sheila, was a daughter of one of the wealthy families."

"I see," she said.

"On the other hand, Mabel, my brother's wife, is the daughter of one of our plant foremen. She left Seven Timbers to attend business school in Boston. She came back and worked in our office, and Ned fell in love with her and married her."

"Quite a romance."

"She's beautiful, but they have no children," Charles said, a slight frown on his handsome face. "I sometimes think that both Ned and I tended to neglect our marriages for the business. It's too late for me to do anything about it, but Ned still can. I'm glad he brought Mabel with him today. She enjoys shopping here."

"You have a son," she said.

"Yes," he said, the shadow remaining on his face. "He is seventeen, and it seems he will never walk again."

"I'm so sorry!"

Charles Prentiss did that thing that Nurse Russell had mentioned to her. He stared beyond her now with a haunted expression in his pale-blue eyes and said, "I have learned to live with it in a sort of way. It's more difficult now that his mother is gone. I took him out hunting with me one day. There was an accident — he was standing on some pulp logs, they rolled out from under him and the gun went off. He might have been killed. As it happened, the bullet struck his spine."

"Nothing can be done for him?"

"He's been to three or four specialists," the man in bed said. "One of them claimed that he should be able to walk with the aid of crutches. I found special, light crutches and had a therapist work with him. He responded for a while and then gave up. Now

26

he uses his wheel chair only."

"That's too bad."

"Especially when you consider that he is only seventeen," the injured man said. "He has a long life ahead of him. Thank goodness he has one consuming interest. He is an avid wireless ham operator. He spends hours at a time sending and receiving messages from all over the world. It seems to somehow compensate him for his crippled state."

She nodded. "I can understand that. And it is good that he has this interest."

"It's his whole life," Charles Prentiss said with a sigh. "I never can forgive myself for what happened. I'm sure he's bitter about it, though nothing is said between us."

"It's not anything you should blame yourself for," she protested.

Charles Prentiss gave her a bleak look. "We've had too many accidents. After a while it becomes difficult to accept them."

"I know," she said with sympathy.

At that moment the doctor arrived. And while he made no mention of her describing the sleeptalking of Charles Prentiss, he did ask the patient a number of questions about how he slept. The end result of the short cross-examination was that the surgeon changed the sedative that the injured man had been taking and substituted a stronger one.

After the doctor left she busied herself with a routine dressing of her patient's injured leg. And before she knew it some time had passed and Ned Prentiss had returned, accompanied by his lovely young wife. Mabel Prentiss had the figure and face of a model, with high cheekbones and a blonde, Nordic beauty. In a dark mink coat and matching hat she made an impressive figure in the austere, white hospital room.

She at once went to Charles' side and kissed him. "How well you are looking!" she exclaimed happily. "I was afraid you would be much worse."

The man in bed smiled grimly. "I'm badly enough off. But I'm going to get out of here soon."

Mabel laughed, showing sparkling, even, white teeth, and said, "I'm sure you will!" And she patted his shoulder with a gloved hand.

During all this Ned Prentiss had stood quietly in the background with a sober look on his plain face, and now he said, "Mrs. Stanley, may I introduce my wife."

Mabel Prentiss studied her with a

smiling glance and said, "So you are the one! My husband has been telling me about you. He's impressed!"

"Only attractive nurse I've got," Charles Prentiss said from his bed.

Ned said, "What time do you take your evening meal, Mrs. Stanley?"

"Whenever it is convenient for the patient," she said.

"I see," the patient's younger brother said. "I have some business details to go over with Charles. They'll only be boring for Mabel. I wonder if you and she mightn't go have your meal together while my brother and I are talking."

The blonde Mabel gave her husband an accusing look. "You just want to be rid of us!"

"That's partly right," her husband said with an easy smile. "But I'd also like you and Mrs. Stanley to know each other better."

"I think it's a good idea," Charles said. And he asked Lucy, "Would that suit you?"

"I have no choice," she said. "I'd just as soon go now as later."

"Fine!" Mabel said briskly. "Then you shall show me the way to the cafeteria, and we'll let these two would-be business tycoons talk about whatever it is they have in mind."

"On your way," her husband said. "I'll want to pick up a bite later at the airport snack bar."

So Lucy found herself escorting the elegantly dressed young woman to the cafeteria, where they attracted a good deal of attention from the staff members there and the visitors at the various tables. It was apparent that the striking, blonde Mabel impressed people wherever she went. She good-naturedly took a place in line with Lucy and handled her tray with dexterity.

When they finally sat down at a table in a far corner Mabel smiled at her and said, "Reminds me of my student days in Boston. We used to have a cafeteria at the school."

Lucy said, "It's an everyday experience for me. I found it a little strange after being away from it during my marriage."

Mabel raised her eyebrows. "You were married?"

"Yes," she said, and she briefly filled the other young woman in on her life story. She ended with, "It seemed natural that I come back to nursing."

"I suppose so," Mabel said, her fork in hand and poised over her plate as she considered this. Her dark-blue eyes had a thoughtful look in them. "I don't know what I'd do if anything happened to Ned or if we should decide to separate. I don't think I'd enjoy being a secretary again."

She smiled at the mink-clad girl. "It's not likely you'll ever be faced with the decision."

Mabel returned to her salad and shrugged. "It's hard to tell. After what happened to Charles, I'm terrified. It could have been Ned, and he might have been killed."

"Such things aren't apt to happen often," she said.

"You can't be sure," Mabel replied, her lovely face showing her apprehensions. "We've had far too many accidents at Seven Timbers." And she went on to explain. "That is the name of our village and also the name of the Prentiss family mansion."

"I see," she said. She recalled Charles having made some mention of this.

"I remember the house when I was a little girl," Mabel said, pausing over her food again. "I was the child of a foreman working in the mill, and that house held a magic for me. I never dreamed I would live there one day. It was a place for the rich. In a world wealthy beyond my imagining."

She studied the blonde's rapt expression.

"And yet you do live there now."

"I do," Mabel said with a quick smile. "And now I take it for granted. I know my father and mother are still impressed. But it doesn't hold any awe for me anymore. In fact, I'm not sure that I'm any happier in Seven Timbers than I was in my father's house. Or that there is that much happiness there for anyone."

"Still, it must be an interesting change in lifestyle," Lucy suggested.

"It is that," the other girl agreed. "Seven Timbers is a great mansion built of logs. You've seen plenty of log cabins, I'm sure. But this is different. It is larger than the biggest lodge you've ever seen. It is built on three different levels, and has a front veranda that overlooks the village and the snow-clad hills beyond and a rear platform high over a rushing stream in the woods."

"It sounds wonderful."

"It has majesty and a beauty of its own," the girl agreed. "On the inside it is finished like any other fine mansion. You'd never think it had a crude log exterior. The boys' grandfather built it, and I must say it suits its location."

"I'm sure it does."

Mabel sat back in her chair with a sigh and seemed to debate sipping her coffee as she stared at the well-filled cup. She said, "We ought all to be having a fine life there. But we're not."

"That's too bad," she said.

"The house has always had more than its share of the tragic," Mabel Prentiss went on. "And lately it has been most frightening. You know that Charles has a son?"

"Yes."

Mabel's lovely face showed sadness. "And you've heard the story of his crippling a few years ago?"

She nodded. "A terrible thing to happen."

"Doubly so because Charles blames himself."

"He oughtn't to!"

"I know, but he does," Mabel said. She gave her a meaningful look and said, "You see, his late wife, Sheila, never forgave him for what happened. She accused him again and again of being responsible for David's crippling."

Lucy frowned and remembered the tortured words of her patient as he'd fought off his nightmares. He had mentioned the name of his son and his wife. No doubt this was what had been tormenting him so.

She said, "That was hardly fair!"

"I agree," the blonde girl opposite her

33

said. "But it was a constant battle between them. I can't tell you how many times I've heard them quarrel about it."

"Did the son know?"

"I'm afraid he overheard the quarrels, and I think he came to blame his father as well. I can only tell you that since his mother's death he has behaved very oddly. He's sullen and aloof with everyone, including his father."

"That is too bad."

Again Mabel's eyes met hers. "You know about the death of Charles' wife?"

"Yes."

"She met her death in a strange way. No one knows what happened. I was visiting a friend's house at the time, the men were all out somewhere. Only David was in the house, and he was in his room working over his wireless set with the door closed. So he heard nothing. But when Charles returned he found Sheila stretched out at the bottom of the steep, lower stairway with her neck broken. They decided she'd tripped. She insisted on wearing high heels even when they weren't fashionable. But it's hard to say."

She stared at the blonde girl. "You mean?"

"I mean no one really knows what happened," Mabel said almost harshly. "But I can tell you one thing. Sheila has tried to come back and let us know what went on that night. I'm sure of that because I have seen her ghost!"

Chapter Two

Lucy heard the blonde girl's words with a distinct feeling of shock. She stared at Mabel Prentiss as she asked, "Do you mean you actually have seen something?"

"Yes," Mabel said evenly. "I know the others scoff at me. But I know what I've seen. One night I came upon her phantom figure in the corridor not far from the head of the stairway where she fell."

"How could you be sure it was her?"

"The phantom suggested Sheila," the blonde girl insisted. "I can't tell you how, but I knew right away. And I have seen shadows in other parts of the house. I'm sure it is Sheila moving about. Things have happened that can't be explained. Items have vanished and then turned up in some other room without any explanation."

"And your answer is that ghosts are at work."

"Yes," Mabel Prentiss said. "Sheila is unhappy in that other world, desperate that we should know the truth about her death."

"But if it were only an unimportant accident, if she merely stumbled, would that be of such concern to her? Why would she wish to contact you?"

The beautiful blonde showed a wise look. "I think there is more than that to it. That is why her spirit roams the house."

"You think she might have been the victim of foul play?" she asked warily.

"I can't be sure," was the other girl's reply. "I don't know what to think. It happened without any witnesses. Who knows what took place that night!"

"That's a very strange story," she said. "How does my patient feel about it?"

"Charles?" the blonde girl said, raising an eyebrow. "I'm sure he still wonders about it. But now he has his own accident to think about."

She gazed at the girl across the table from her. "Yes. You were there when that happened, weren't you?"

Mabel crimsoned. "Who told you that?"

"He did."

"Really?" Mabel appeared a trifle surprised. Then quickly recovering her usual poise, she said carelessly, "It is a fact. I was there on the platform with him when he toppled over. I was shocked."

"You didn't expect it."

"Of course not," the blonde young woman said. "Charles is so familiar with everything about the mill. It still puzzles me."

"I see," she said quietly.

Mabel gave her another appraising look. "You are really interested in my brother-in-law and his background, aren't you?"

It was her turn to blush. She said, "I hope I haven't seemed too curious, but I do take an interest in all my patients."

"You should," the other girl agreed. "I'm glad Charles has someone like you as a nurse. The other ones I've met have seemed over-age and jaded."

"Many of the private duty nurses are older," she agreed. "But I'm sure they do take an interest in their patients, even though they may not seem to."

"Probably," Mabel Prentiss said. "It's too bad David won't come down to see his father. He has a compact, folding wheelchair and we could easily bring him here. But he won't come. The truth is he cares more about that wireless room of his than he does about his father."

"He is young," Lucy said. "And the wireless has come to mean a great deal to him."

"He's the world's most enthusiastic ham radio operator," the blonde young woman agreed. "He spends most of his days and nights in there at the set. I think he gives too much of his time to it."

"Perhaps as he grows older he'll find other interests," she suggested.

Mabel Prentiss rolled her eyes. "I wouldn't want to count on it. We're a strange, isolated household in a strange, isolated region. As a family group I think we are at a loss. Ned and Charles have little in common aside from the operating of the mills."

"That is often the way with brothers."

"Probably. But when we all live under the same roof it is a little odd. Ned, my husband, is an outdoor type. Fishing and hunting are his chief interests, while Charles prefers to read and is interested in music and art. Sheila was an excellent artist. The house is filled with her paintings."

"I didn't know."

"Oh, yes. That is how she and Charles met. He visited a one-man show she was having at the university. It was love at first sight. She continued to paint through the years, though she offered little to the market. She always painted a few hours each day. She had a studio in the attic of Seven Timbers. Charles locked it up after her death."

"That's interesting."

"He was very badly shaken by her accidental death. He goes up there every so often and sits alone in the studio. I've argued with him about it. I'm not at all certain it's healthy for him to live on memories of the dead."

She said, "Perhaps he enjoys the quiet up there and studying the work she left. It may not be so unhealthy."

"Perhaps not," Mabel Prentiss said reluctantly. It was evident that she thought otherwise. "Then there's John Rhode. He's the older brother of Sheila. He has his own house next to ours and lives there alone with a housekeeper. Before Sheila's death he used to come to visit us a great deal. But he's keeping to himself lately."

"The Rhode family were wealthy, weren't they?"

"They *are* wealthy!" Mabel said with emphasis. "Sheila could never forget that. She always let me know that her family rated far above mine in the village, even though we'd married brothers. I often laughed at her airs!"

Lucy was embarrassed, as she could see

the blonde girl felt strongly on this point. She was sorry she'd brought it up, and she quickly said, "Perhaps you just imagined it."

"Never," the Nordic-type beauty shook her head. "I knew when she patronized me, and I didn't really mind. Ned and I have a better marriage than she and Charles ever had. She acted as she did mostly through insecurity."

"Many people are driven by their own inner fears," Lucy said.

"John Rhode, her brother, is different. He behaves like the true aristocrat. He's always known wealth and he accepts it very casually."

"He is active in the lumbering business, too?"

"Yes. He sold out his own mills to the Prentiss Company. And now he has a small share in our operations. But he travels a lot and lets Charles and Ned do most of the actual management."

She smiled ruefully. "So this John Rhode is a sort of gentleman of leisure."

"To a great extent. He also is interested in the arts and he reads a lot. There isn't all that much to do up there! We do get some Canadian television and radio, but a lot of it is in the French language."

"You are very close to Quebec."

Mabel smiled. "Yes. I enjoy shopping in Montreal and Boston. If we didn't have the planes at our disposal to get us away quickly, I'd go berserk."

"I imagine it can be lonely."

"You don't really know until you've lived there."

"But you should be used to it. You grew up there," Lucy said.

The blonde's face shadowed. "I doubt that I'll ever get used to it or like it."

"That's strange."

"Not really," Mabel Prentiss said. "Most country people are attracted to the city and vice versa." She glanced at her wristwatch. "It's getting late. We must go. Ned will be waiting for me."

"I'm sorry," she apologized. "I allowed us to talk too long."

"No!" Mabel said. "I've enjoyed every minute of it. I have few other women of my own age to talk to. And it may help you understand Charles better as a patient to know something about his background."

"I'm certain it will," she said as they got up from the table in the cafeteria.

Back in the private room Ned Prentiss was waiting somewhat impatiently. He bade Lucy and his brother a quick

42

goodbye and hurried off with his mink-clad blonde wife. When Lucy found herself alone in the room with her patient, she saw that he was smiling at her from his propped-up position in the bed.

"What do you think of Mabel?" he asked.

"She's beautiful," Lucy said carefully. "And she seems very intelligent."

"She's both of those things," Charles Prentiss said with a wise look on his handsome face. "And she likes to talk a lot. I'm sure you noticed that."

"Yes."

He shook his head. "Sheila used to be upset by Mabel's desire to gossip. I tried to tell my wife it was mostly because Mabel was lonely, but she didn't quite believe it."

"I can imagine that she has a lonely life."

"Ned gives her everything she asks for," the man in the bed said. "They have no children, and I'm sure they miss that. But she goes to Montreal and Boston a lot. There's no reason for her to be lonely. Sheila loved Seven Timbers. Its scenery fed her art talent."

"Mabel told me your late wife painted very well."

Charles Prentiss looked pleased. "I think she did. Most of her paintings were oils, and many of them were landscapes. I'd say

43

she excelled at landscapes."

"How sad that she died so young."

His handsome face shadowed. "Yes. It was a tragedy," he agreed.

Then he changed the subject and began to talk to her about Seven Timbers, both the village and the house. He lost himself in his enthusiastic description of the mountains, snowcapped and tipped with evergreens. His account of the vast snow-covered fields and the great forests adjoining them held her enthralled. She could tell that he loved the North country and the lumbering in which he was engaged.

When she gave him the new medication that night, he slept soundly. And when she returned to take over her shift with him the next day, he seemed much more rested and a great deal improved. Even his doctor commented on this. It was the beginning of a long period of improvement in which she came to know her patient very well and admire him. And in keeping busy with him she forgot much of her own loneliness and sorrow.

By the last of January Charles Prentiss was able to walk about the hospital corridors with the aid of a cane. He would need the cane for several months longer, but the surgeon had assured him that eventually his leg would be as good as before the accident. It was at this time that Lucy somewhat embarrassedly suggested to him that he no longer needed her. He'd already dispensed with his day and night nurse, and it was beginning to cause raised eyebrows at the head nurse's desk that she had still been retained.

His brother and Mabel had paid a brief visit the previous day, and the blonde girl had expressed surprise at seeing her in the room and said, "You're not still on the case?"

She'd crimsoned and said, "Yes. But I won't be much longer."

So now as soon as she'd arrived she'd spoken to Charles Prentiss on the subject. "You don't need a private nurse any longer," she told him.

Charles had been standing in pajamas and dressing gown staring out the window, and resting his weight on his cane. Now he turned to her with a look of wistfulness on his handsome face. "I've been waiting for you to say that," he admitted.

"I don't want us to become a scandal on the floor," she said with good humor.

He smiled thinly. "And I heard Mabel challenge you about being here when she called yesterday. You can always count on her to interfere."

"I had to discuss this with you anyway," she said. "So please don't blame her."

"I won't," he said, turning to her. His blue eyes fixed on her soberly. "You must know why I've kept you on."

"Because you are lonely," she said. "But you'll be leaving the hospital in a few days and so you won't need me."

"That's where you're all wrong," the handsome man said, limping over to face her. "I never thought the day would come when I'd try to prolong my stay in a hospital. But that's what has happened. I've tried to keep on here as long as possible. And because of you!"

"Because of me?" she repeated faintly.

"Yes," his tone was earnest. "You'll have to forgive me, Lucy. I don't mean to take advantage of my position as your patient, but the truth is I've fallen in love with you!"

She stared at him. "I don't believe it!"

"You must!" he insisted. "It's true."

"But you've only known me a few weeks," she protested. "And not as a person, but as a nurse. How much do you really know about me?"

"Enough!" Charles said. "Enough so that I don't want to go back to Seven Timbers without you! Will you marry me, Lucy?"

46

She gasped. The whole thing was much more than she'd bargained for. And she shook her head and said, "I've never thought about you that way!"

He took her by the arm with his free hand and sternly asked, "Can you deny that we get along wonderfully well?"

"No!"

"Do you find me repulsive?"

"Of course not!"

"Is it a life of isolation in the North-woods you fear?"

"No!"

"Well then?" he waited for her answer.

She looked up at him with a bewildered gentleness and said, "It's just that it's all so unexpected!"

"If we hadn't met as patient and nurse but as friends we'd likely have declared our feelings long before this," he protested.

"Perhaps."

"I'm in love with you and I think you're in love with me, Lucy. I have to go back to Seven Timbers. There isn't all that much time. I'd like you to make up your mind and marry me and go back with me as my bride."

"There are so many things to consider!" she protested. "And people! Your son for one! He may not like me!"

"He either will or he won't," Charles said grimly. "I'm not at all certain he likes me. So don't allow that to bother you."

"Ned and Mabel," she said. "What about them? They'll think I threw myself at you."

"They know better than that," he told her. "And they know I would never ask you to marry me unless I made up my own mind about you! Decided that I really cared."

She shook her head in helpless indecision. She knew that she had secretly been dreading the moment when they would have to part. She had come to care for him far too much. And yet she felt that she must be the one to consider it all clearly and not rush into anything that they both might regret later.

She said, "I don't know what to say!"

"I will answer for you," he told her. And he drew her to him and held her close as he kissed her.

As their lips met in a warm caressing she knew that no matter how much she might go on protesting, it had been decided. And she clung to the handsome lumberman knowing that once again in her life she had been fortunate to find a haven of true love.

From that afternoon her life moved at a

hectic pace. Charles Prentiss at once had himself discharged from the hospital and took a motel room in downtown Portland. He phoned Ned and Mabel and informed them that they were taking out a license to marry and requested the couple's presence to stand up with them at the private wedding.

She never did hear exactly what his brother and sister-in-law had said. But whether they were all that pleased or not, they did show up for the ceremony. It seemed to her that Mabel was a good deal less friendly toward her than when they'd met at the hospital and Ned also showed restraint in his manner. However, she overlooked this and put it down to possible nervousness on the part of her new in-laws. If Charles was aware of it, he gave not a hint of it to her.

Following a quiet, civil ceremony she and Charles went to Montreal to honeymoon for a few days. Then they took one of the company planes back to Seven Timbers. Ben Huggard, the young man who acted as company pilot, greeted them at the plane. He was a stocky, tanned type with a round, jolly face and shrewd gray eyes.

"Afternoon folks," he said offhandedly.

"We better get on our way as soon as possible. There's a snowstorm coming up."

"All right, Ben," Charles said, leaning on his cane and then turning to her with a smile. "I want you to meet my wife, Lucy. This is Ben Huggard. He grew up in Seven Timbers and left to work for a commercial airline. Now he's back home working for us."

"Pleased to meet you," Ben said, smiling as he shook her hand. "You can't beat the life of a company pilot. And I like Seven Timbers."

"I hope my wife will," Charles Prentiss said.

"I'm looking forward to going there," she said. And it was true. All the descriptions she'd heard of the rugged country had made her more eager to see it and be part of it. She knew that her husband was unlikely to be happy anywhere else and so she was content to make it her home.

She listened while pilot Ben Huggard and her husband went on talking about the weather and other matters and tried to make up her mind about the stocky Ben. There was no question that he had charm, but there was also a certain coarse familiarity in his manner toward them that made her wonder. She felt guilty because of her misgivings, but she had a suspicion that he regarded the Prentiss family with a certain easy contempt. And she could not help wondering why.

Because of the pilot's warnings they lost no time entering the large private plane and getting under way. As they left the Montreal airport she and Charles sat holding hands and gazing down at the city and river gradually vanishing beneath them on this dull, gray winter day. Soon they were above the first cloud layer and all took on a look of sameness about them.

Ben Huggard, his back to them, kept busy with the dials of the plane. She was startled by the noise of the engines, which were louder than in a regular airline plane. But she and Charles managed to communicate easily by raising their voices. After a little they sat back and relaxed in silence as the plane roared on.

Now that she was nearing Seven Timbers she began to have all the old fears again. She worried about how her new husband's seventeen-year-old crippled son would receive her, and she also was uneasy about the reception she might get from Ned and Mabel. Mabel had been mistress of the big lodge since the death of Sheila and she might well resent giving up that

51

role of authority. And she suddenly recalled Mabel's claim that she'd seen Sheila's
ghost. An unhappy business in itself!

After an hour or so the plane began to
descend. Darkness had come and she was
unable to see anything at first. Then she
saw the rows of lights that marked the private landing field. After circling the field
once the light plane settled down in a
bumpy landing. It streaked ahead for a distance before it came to a halt.

Ben Huggard turned and said, "Sorry it
had to be so rough. It's snowing outside."

"I had an idea it was," Charles said. And
he offered her a smile of apology. "Sorry to
introduce you to the village in such
weather."

"I enjoy a snowstorm," she said.

Ben Huggard opened the door for them
and they got out. Charles helped her down
onto the snowy ground just as a set of ap-
proaching headlights glared through the
darkness.

"That's probably Ned," her husband
said.

But when the Jeep station wagon came
up by them it was someone else who got
out. He wore a short red jacket and a red
cap, with a peak to match, and had a gaunt
yet very intelligent face. He said, "I was al-

most late. Ned couldn't make it, as he's expecting an important phone call, so he asked if I would pick you up."

"Oh?" Charles sounded mildly surprised. And he turned to her and said, "This is our good neighbor, John Rhode, Lucy. I'm glad to have you two meet."

She shook hands with the youngish man with the thin, clever face and said, "Charles has often spoken about you."

"Really?" John Rhode had a pleasant voice. "I'm very happy to meet you. We're so isolated here that an interesting addition to the community means a great deal."

She smiled. "I'm not sure I'm all that interesting."

"I'm certain you are," John Rhode said. "I'll get your bags from the plane and we'll have you back to Seven Timbers in no time."

After the luggage had been transferred from the plane to the Jeep, they began the drive back through the snowstorm. It was coming down so heavily it was almost impossible to see in places.

All three sat in the front seat of the Jeep, with Lucy in the middle. Charles asked the man at the wheel, "How long has it been snowing?"

"More than an hour," John Rhode said.

"I began to worry whether you'd make it or not. I sort of thought you'd wait in Montreal until it cleared."

"You know Ben Huggard," her husband said. "He's ready to fly in almost any kind of weather."

"All right as long as his luck holds out," the man at the wheel said grimly.

They drove for a bit then Charles touched her shoulder and said, "Look directly ahead!"

She did and after a moment was able to make out a huge black bulk with some lights showing at various windows. The snow came in great gusts and cut off her vision for a few seconds, and then she saw the great lodge in which the Prentiss family lived more clearly. Perhaps it was because of the storm, she thought, but it struck her that the log mansion had a rather sinister look.

John Rhode brought the station wagon to a halt by the main, verandahed entrance to the imposing log mansion. But after helping them inside with their bags, he beat a hasty retreat, once again expressing his pleasure at meeting her. So this was the brother of the dead Sheila, Lucy realized, and it seemed to her that he had been friendly enough to her.

The main living room of the lodge opened off the entrance, and its ceiling rose two stories high. There was a balcony at the rear wall and stairways on either side to it. She guessed that the balcony gave access to the bedrooms, and so, it turned out, it did. A chandelier built on the frame of an extra-large, ancient wagon-wheel hung from the ceiling, and its circle of bulbs cast a gentle glow over the big area. At one end of the room a stone fireplace, with a blazing fire in it, rose to the ceiling.

Charles carried her bags up the left stairway, and she went up after him. They reached the balcony and he kept striding on ahead in the dark corridor. At last they came to an open doorway, and he went in and placed the bags on suitable chairs. The bedroom was large, with two oversize beds, and it also had a fireplace with a fire in it.

She smiled at her new husband and said, "It's a marvelous house!"

"You've seen very little of it," he assured her with a subdued smile of his own. There seemed suddenly to be a strangely drawn cast to his face. In the soft light of the bedroom his handsome features had a gaunt look.

She went to him solicitously and said, "Your leg! You didn't use your cane after you got off the plane, and you carried those heavy bags up the stairs!"

"That did me no harm!" he said almost gruffly.

"It could easily," she warned him. "I don't know why I didn't think myself. I guess it was the excitement of coming into the house. You must find your cane and use it. And no more lifting of bags!"

He smiled thinly. "I see I have a nurse again!"

"You need one," she rebuked him.

He touched his lips to her forehead and said, "I'll let you unpack and I'll go see my son. I'll also speak to the cook about fixing us some dinner and see if I can locate Ned and Mabel."

She suddenly realized they hadn't been in evidence to greet her and said, "Perhaps they've gone out somewhere."

"That is highly unlikely," he said in a taut voice. "You go ahead and make yourself comfortable. I won't be long."

He left her and she made a more thorough study of the room, with its fine antique chests of drawers. There was a bathroom attached to the room and several large closets. She at once opened her suitcases and began taking out her things. This task occupied her for almost twenty minutes, and still Charles had not returned. She now began to feel somewhat uneasy, and so she decided to leave the room and explore the great lodge by herself.

She followed along the corridor without meeting anyone. Then she crossed the balcony and tried the other corridor. From far down it she heard the sound of voices. She followed the sound and gradually recognized that it was someone carrying on a conversation over a ham wireless transmitter. When she reached the door of the room from which the sound was coming, it was partly open. She looked in and saw a young man in a wheelchair, with his back to her, bent over the table from which the equipment rose to the ceiling. He had earphones on and was sending call letters.

She went into the room and stood for a moment. All at once the youth in the wheelchair turned and saw her. He took off his headphones and ceased his performance at the wireless set. She was touched by his resemblance to Charles. He had his father's features, though he was of smaller build, and there was a frail look about him.

She broke the silence between them, saying, "Hello. I'm Lucy. I guess your father has told you about me."

The youth with the curly golden hair

eyed her sullenly. He said stiffly, "Yes, he did."

She forced a smile. "I hope we can be good friends, David."

"Does that make any difference?"

"It does for me," she said. "I don't want to come here as an intruder."

"I don't like to be interrupted when I'm sending and getting messages," he said.

"I'm sorry," she apologized. "I won't come in again when you are busy. I didn't understand."

David's young face still remained sullen. But he said, "It's all right."

"I wonder where your father is?" she asked.

"He left here about five minutes ago," David said. "Maybe he is downstairs."

"Thanks," she said. "I'll look for him."

David eyed her with disdain. "You aren't going to like it here," was his warning.

She felt her cheeks warm with embarrassment. And she said, "Why do you say that?"

"Wait and see," was his enigmatic reply, and he turned his back on her and put on the headphones again. It was a clear message of dismissal that she could not ignore.

She wheeled around quickly and left the room with a feeling of humiliation. Her new stepson had plainly indicated that he resented her appearance in the house. He'd also shown that he would do nothing to make it pleasant for her. She had expected some resentment from the youth, but nothing like this.

Making her way downstairs she came face to face with Ned as he appeared through the door of a side room. He at once looked embarrassed and nodded to her.

"You did get here," he said by way of greeting her. "Sorry I couldn't make it to the airport."

"I know," she said. "John Rhode explained. You were waiting for an important phone call."

"Yes," her husband's younger brother said, standing there looking rather guilty. "Well, what do you make of the place? Does it live up to your expectations?"

"It's very interesting," she said. "A truly unique house."

"No question of that," Ned Prentiss agreed. "And the surrounding area is pleasant. When the storm is over in the morning, you'll be able to appreciate it."

"Yes. I expect so," she said. "Have you seen Charles?"

"He went to the kitchen," Ned said. "He ought to be here in a moment."

The wind, howling around the log mansion, could be heard plainly in the big living room. She gave a tiny shudder. "It sounds as if the storm may have become worse."

"It has," he agreed. "You were lucky to make a safe landing."

"I begin to think so," she said. "Where is Mabel?"

Ned's face flushed. "She has a headache," he said. "She is subject to them. She asked me to make her excuses. She planned to welcome you with a special dinner."

"That was kind of her," she said, playing along with him. "I quite understand."

He nodded nervously. "Well, good to have you here. I'd better go up and see how she is."

"Don't let me keep you," she said.

"Thanks," Ned said. "I'll see you in the morning."

He went on upstairs and vanished down one of the dark corridors. She crossed to the log fire in the great stone fireplace and stared into its flaming depths. It began to seem that with the exception of her new husband no one wanted her in the log mansion. While David had been open in voicing his dislike of her coming, the others were showing it in a more veiled fashion. But that did not change the facts.

She heard a step behind her and turned to see her husband. He came up and said, "Mrs. Warren, the housekeeper, is setting the table in the dining room for us this very minute."

"I'm sorry to be such a nuisance."

Her husband's handsome face showed annoyance. "You mustn't feel that way. She doesn't mind."

She said, "You're still not using your cane."

"I seem to be able to manage well enough without it."

"You may get some bad effects in the morning," she warned him.

"Let me take that chance," he said obstinately.

She shrugged. "You didn't come back for me, so I took a look around the house on my own."

"I guessed that when I saw you standing here," he said.

Her eyes met his. "I found David's wireless room and spoke with him for a moment."

"Did you?" he asked stiffly, the reflection of the flames from the fireplace playing a pattern on his handsome face.

"Yes." She paused. "He doesn't like me, Charles."

"Nonsense!" her husband expostulated. "The boy doesn't know you! How can he make a judgment?"

"He hated me on sight," she said. "I could tell. I tried to get through to him, but I'm afraid he's made up his mind to shut off my wave length. I'm sorry."

"Give him time," Charles said with a frown. "I only regret you went in there tonight. You mustn't try to rush him. He's a very strange boy."

"I realize now I made a mistake," she said. "I was stupid."

"It doesn't matter," he said wearily and took her in his arms. "As long as we're happy, the rest will work out."

"I hope so," she said with a sigh. "Neither Ned nor Mabel were here to greet me. But of course they have good excuses. Ned told me a moment ago about his wife's headache spells."

"She does have headaches," Charles told her. "You must believe that."

She smiled wanly. "What choice have I?"

"Let us go in to dinner," he urged her, taking her by the arm. "You'll feel better when you've had something to eat."

Lucy allowed him to lead her to the large dining room, where the cook had set out a sumptuous buffet on a candlelit table.

They were able to sit comfortably and serve themselves without any interruptions. They chatted quietly and she did feel better for the food and drink. David sat on one side of the long table and she sat at the end near him. There were several open doorways into the room, with shadowy corridors behind them. She knew that one of them led to the kitchen, but she had no clear idea about the other ones.

Charles told her, "My late father enlarged this house from the first log structure put up by my grandfather. So it has stood here for almost a hundred years."

She had her tea cup in hand, and was about to ask him where John Rhode's house was located, when suddenly in the doorway at the other end of the room a shadowy female form appeared. It was a figure exactly like the one that Mabel had described to her as the phantom form of Sheila. It lurked in the shadows with its face hidden. The sight of it brought the story vividly to her, and she dropped her tea cup and cried out in alarm!

Chapter Three

Charles jumped to his feet with a startled look on his handsome face. "What is wrong?" he exclaimed.

Her face pale, she pointed to the doorway. "There!"

He frowned and turned to see what it was she meant. And it was no surprise to her that there was now nothing to see. The phantom figure in the shadows had vanished.

He glanced back at her again. "I see nothing!"

"It's gone."

"What's gone?"

She gave him a pathetic look. "A figure in the shadows. I saw it move!"

He eyed her incredulously. "What sort of figure?"

"I don't know exactly," she admitted. "I think it was a woman with some sort of scarf on her head."

Charles stared at her and then turned

and went to the doorway and out. He returned after a moment, saying, "There isn't a sign of anyone out there. It's a passage leading to the rear stairway, so none of the kitchen help would show themselves there. You must have been imagining things!"

"No!" she protested.

"I'm sorry," he said, coming up to her. "I know your coming here hasn't been pleasant. You've been under a strain. It's natural that a shadow should frighten you."

She was on her feet now. "I don't think it was a shadow."

"What else?"

"I don't know," she was forced to admit. Better than trying to convince him it had been the ghost of his first wife. Let it rest. She was too weary to argue.

Her handsome husband stared at her and sighed. "I think it is time we went to bed."

She bowed her head. "Very well," she said.

They left the candlelight of the dining room and mounted the stairway of the great lodge. The wind still could be heard howling outside, and hail clattered against the windows. She now came to fully realize the isolation of this new home of hers and the cruel fury of the weather in the North country in which it was located. She felt as if she had traveled back into another century.

Long after they were in bed and the lights had been turned off she listened to the storm and thought about the phantom she had seen. For she was convinced it had been a phantom. The wind shrieked eerily, and once she thought she heard a woman's voice pleading and screaming in it. And she knew she was afraid and that her fears might continue to torment her as long as she remained at Seven Timbers.

When she awoke the next morning, the sun was shining in through the windows, and she saw the covers had been thrown back on her husband's bed and it was empty. All the experiences of the previous night came crowding into her mind and she wondered where Charles might be. She rose and quickly washed and dressed and went downstairs.

A prim woman with short gray hair and hornrimmed glasses greeted her in the dining room. "You must be the new Mrs. Prentiss," the thin woman said. "And I'm Mrs. Warren, the housekeeper."

"I'm happy to meet you," she said,

standing by the table. "Have you any idea where my husband might be?"

"He and his brother have gone to the mill," the prim woman explained. "We start work early in these parts."

"So it seems," she said.

"If you'll sit down, I'll see you're served breakfast," Mrs. Warren said. "No doubt the other Mrs. Prentiss will soon be down to join you."

"Does she have breakfast about this time?"

"Yes. She comes down later than the men folks every morning," Mrs. Warren said. "And young David has his meals taken to him upstairs."

"I see," she said.

"I'll be happy to take you on a tour of the lodge whenever you like," the prim woman said. "The other Mrs. Prentiss told me you would be taking charge of the household affairs."

She sat at the table. "There's lots of time for that. I'm quite satisfied to have her continue taking care of things."

Mrs. Warren's prim face was stony. She said, "But the other Mrs. Prentiss said you'd be taking over at once."

"Well, I'll see about it," she said. "You can send me in breakfast. And I'd like a cup of coffee first, if you don't mind."

"Yes, Mrs. Prentiss. I'll tell the girl," the prim woman said, and left the dining room.

Lucy was almost finished with breakfast when the blonde and beautiful Mabel came in to sit at the table with her. The blonde eyed her and said, "You look very well this morning. Not at all tired from your trip."

"It wasn't all that long," she said.

"No, but the storm was dreadful," Mabel said. And she ordered her breakfast from the maid who was serving them. After this was attended to, she told Lucy, "I'm sorry I wasn't on hand to greet you last night. I did have a wretched headache."

"Please don't apologize," she told her.

Mabel was studying her now to the point where it made her feel uncomfortable. At last the blonde said, "You know I was surprised when you decided to marry Charles."

"It was a sudden decision," she admitted.

"I didn't mean that," the blonde girl said. "I was thinking more of the hazards of marrying him."

"The hazards?"

"Yes," Mabel said. "David, for instance. He is incensed at the idea of anyone taking his mother's place."

"I wouldn't try to do that," she replied. "At the very best I can only be an older friend to him."

Mabel smiled grimly. "David doesn't see it that way. And to make it worse there's his resentment against his father for the accident that crippled him. I blame Sheila for planting that bad seed in his mind."

"Terribly unfair of her."

"She could be unfair when she liked," was Mabel's dry comment. "But don't try to convince David of that."

"I won't try to convince him of anything."

"That would be wise," Mabel agreed. "Another hazard of your marriage is this place. It is so remote and wild. And both Charles and Ned give far too much of their time to the business."

"You think so?"

"No one is in a place to know better," Mabel said ruefully. "I would have warned you if you'd asked me."

"It never occurred to me that I should need a warning."

Mabel eyed her directly. "And on top of everything else, this house is haunted. Haunted by Sheila's unhappy spirit. I remember telling you that."

She felt a chill surge through her as she

thought of the previous night. Involuntarily she lifted her eyes to stare at the doorway in which she had been so certain she'd seen the phantom figure. The doorway was no longer shadowed now.

Mabel frowned. "Why are you staring at that doorway?"

She looked at the Nordic-type beauty and said, "It was your mention of the phantom."

"Oh?"

"Last night I was certain I saw the figure you described standing in that doorway watching me."

Mabel's eyebrows rose. "That makes sense," she said. "Of course Sheila's phantom would wish to study you on the sly."

"I complained to Charles. But by that time there was nothing there. The phantom had vanished."

"That doesn't surprise me," the other girl said. "Though I am certain that Charles didn't want to believe you."

"He didn't."

"Don't ever expect him to," Mabel warned her curtly. "It is part of his guilt complex that he won't accept that Sheila returns here in spirit form."

She was puzzled. "Why should he feel guilty about it?"

The blonde looked enigmatic. She shrugged. "Your guess is as good as mine."

"When I saw the shadow I remembered your story," she said.

"Of course you would," Mabel said in a satisfied voice. "And you'd better be prepared for more manifestations. I know they will come."

"You really think so?"

"I know so," the blonde young woman said soberly. "I have seen Sheila's ghost in the shadows many times. But no one really believes me."

"Charles didn't believe me," she lamented.

"You'll get used to that."

"Oh?" She was prepared for Mabel to show pessimism, but this was stronger than she expected.

"Things have happened here that have no reasonable explanation," the blonde girl went on. She was clearly enjoying making a case against the lodge and Lucy's marriage.

"Tell me," she begged her.

"You'll find out," was Mabel's reply.

She said, "Mrs. Warren spoke to me about taking over the house affairs. I really feel they should be left in your hands. You have been running things all along."

"No," Mabel said. "I want you to be responsible. As the wife of the older brother, it is your place. Sheila was in charge when I came here."

"There's no need to stay with that!" she protested.

"Charles will be angry if you don't," the other girl made a prediction.

"You think that?"

"I do."

"I can't manage without your help," she protested.

"Mrs. Warren will give you all the help you need," was the blonde young woman's reply. "As a matter of fact, she takes care of most of the day-to-day details for me."

Lucy felt sure this was right, and it seemed that Mabel was not interested in the nominal role of mistress of the household any longer. So she said, "Very well. I'll talk to her."

She finished her coffee and saw that Mabel was still only partway through her breakfast. Sitting back from the table she asked the blonde girl, "Don't the men leave here awfully early?"

Mabel grimaced. "A family tradition. They open the mill at seven. But then they close it at four, so they have a long time to themselves in the late afternoon and evening."

"I see."

"If it weren't that I get away occasionally, I'd go out of my mind," Mabel said with disgust. "And Ned refuses to accompany me unless he has some business to attend to. You'll do better with Charles. He isn't so stubborn that way. I think he enjoys having an occasional holiday away from here!"

"I certainly hope so," she said.

The blonde girl smiled at her acidly over her coffee. "I wonder how long it will be before you begin wishing you were back working at the Portland Hospital."

"I hope that never happens."

"Don't count on it," was Mabel's rather amazing reply.

She left the dining room while the blonde girl was still at the table. When she went upstairs the first person she met in the corridor was David, coming along at a fast pace in his wheelchair. When he saw her his face took on a stolid expression.

She halted in his way to say, "Hello, David, I'm glad to see you."

"Yeah?" he said in a bored tone.

"Remember," she said, "we may not always agree but I would like to be your friend."

His boyish face was grim with rejection as he said, "I have all the friends I need without adding any." And he wheeled the chair on, forcing her to step aside and give way to him.

The encounter had been humiliating for her. It was in essence another defeat. But she didn't mean to allow herself to be too discouraged. She would continue trying to win David over, and surely he would one day recognize that she only wanted to be as good to him as he would allow her to be.

In her room she gazed out the window and saw the nearby mill buildings and the village, which was about two miles down the hillside. Seven Timbers had the distinction of being high on a hill with an excellent view of everything. On this morning after the storm the fields were gleaming white and the great evergreens showed a white mantle.

As she watched she saw sleighs drawn by teams of horses and carrying great logs to the mills to be transformed into finished wood for construction. The tinkle of the sleigh bells cut through the crisp morning air and could actually be heard inside the lodge. It was like a Christmas card scene come alive.

She moved away from the window and gave her attention to their bedroom. And it was then that she saw the many paintings on the walls, the majority of them land-scapes of the area in all the four seasons signed by Sheila. It was a strange experience studying the paintings, like going over a message left by a dead person. Each of the paintings was meant to express some mood or scene, and she was impressed by the talent of her husband's first wife.

Before leaving the room and going to speak with Mrs. Warren about the assumption of the household affairs, she went to her dresser to straighten it out a little and lock her jewel case. And there among her own jewelry was a pearl pin she'd never seen before!

It was a startling experience! She gazed down at the pearl pin with a kind of dismay. And it took her a full moment or two before she found herself able to touch it. When she did pick it up and saw that it was an expensive piece, her hand trembled. She hurried to lock up her own things, and then with the pearl pin in the pocket of her pantsuit she went out to try to find Mabel.

She reached the balcony and saw the blonde beauty coming up the left stairway with a bored expression on her lovely face. She waited until Mabel had reached the balcony before going to her and saying, "I need some information from you."

Mabel stared at her. "All right."

She produced the pin. "Have you seen this before?"

Mabel looked astonished and then took it from her. She said in an awed tone, "It's the lost pin!"

"What does that mean?"

The blonde looked at her. "When Sheila died this valuable pin was missing. Charles looked for it everywhere and couldn't find it. And now it turns up. Where did you find it?"

She swallowed hard. "With my jewelry."

"You must be joking!"

"No. I found it there just now. Where could it have come from?"

Mabel studied the expensive pin as it lay on the palm of her hand. "There can only be two explanations, and it has to be one or the other."

"Name them."

"Easy. Either Charles found the pin without mentioning it to anyone and left it there for you, or —" At this point she hesitated.

"Or what?"

Mabel gave her a knowing look. "Or she left it there for you."

"She?"

"You know who," Mabel said. And to

pound her point home she nodded at one of Sheila's paintings on the wall of the balcony.

"You can't mean that!" she protested.

"But I do," Mabel said with an almost triumphant smile. "I warned you that strange things happen here. This is a typical example of them." And she handed the pin back to Lucy.

She took it with a troubled expression and put it back in the pocket of her brown knit pantsuit again. She said, "I'll speak to Charles. He must have put it there."

"Do!" Mabel urged her. "And I'll be interested to hear what he tells you about it." With that she continued on along the corridor.

Lucy was left alone on the balcony. She grasped the railing and gazed down into the huge living room with its many expensive scatter rugs and fine pieces of furniture. And she saw that all the walls were filled with paintings done by Charles' first wife. She was literally surrounded by the influence of the dead woman!

How could she have allowed herself to become involved in such a situation? She ought to have known better. But she had allowed her loneliness and her love for Charles to sway her. Now she was seeing what this decision she had made meant. Yet she was prepared to fight against it all to keep the love of the man she'd married and give them at least some small share of happiness. She knew it wouldn't be easy, but it would be nothing less than utter cowardice to desert Charles now. No wonder he had been so strangely tense last night. He'd known better than she what they were facing.

She found her eyes moving to the stairway at her left and then the one at her right. From all the accounts that she'd heard it seemed certain that Sheila had met her death on either one or the other of the two stairways. She saw that the fall was definitely long enough to cause a fatal injury if one should be so unfortunate as to fall all the way. And it seemed that this was what had happened to Charles' first wife.

There was a movement down below, and she saw that Mrs. Warren was standing there staring up at her in her usual prim fashion. The gray-haired woman with the hornrimmed glasses asked her, "Are you ready to have me show you through the lodge now, Mrs. Prentiss?"

"Yes," she said in a quiet voice. "Yes. I suppose you may as well."

"Thank you," the prim woman said,

sounding pleased. She came up the stairs and joined her.

Lucy asked her, "Which of these stairways did the first Mrs. Prentiss fall down?"

Her question at once put the prim woman's face in shadow. She gave a fearful glance at the stairway on the right. She said, "It was that one! I'll never forget it!"

"Did you find her?" she asked.

"You might say so," the housekeeper told her. "Though Mr. Charles arrived just as I discovered her. So you could say we found her at about the same time."

"I see," she said. "And she was dead then?"

"Broke her neck, poor dear!" Mrs. Warren said bitterly. "And her with so much talent!" She indicated the paintings with a sweep of her hand.

"Yes. That's true."

"And the boy needing her so! Poor crippled David!"

Limply she said, "I know. It was a tragedy."

"Believe me, I would never have mentioned it if you hadn't been the one to bring it up first," the housekeeper said.

"I understand that."

There was sympathy in the eyes behind the hornrimmed glasses. "I would be the last to try and hurt you or anyone else."

"I'm sure you would," she agreed.

Mrs. Warren glanced toward the stairway of death again and gave a tiny shudder. "I wish I could forget that night, but I can't. I wake up sometimes after having nightmares about it."

"I'm sorry," she said. "How do you think it happened?"

"She must have stumbled," Mrs. Warren said.

"But what would cause her to stumble?" she persisted.

The prim woman took on an almost frightened look. "I don't know."

"She would be familiar with the stairway?"

"Yes."

"And the lights were on, I assume."

"They were."

"And yet she stumbled so badly that she fell the whole length of the stairway. It doesn't seem logical."

"Many things that happen aren't logical," Mrs. Warren said with a shake of her head.

"True," she agreed. "I suppose it could have been her shoes, since she was presumably wearing high heels."

"Yes, madam. I warned her against

them, but she didn't listen. She was a fine woman but she had a mind of her own."

"So I have been told."

"Well, it's all at an end now," Mrs. Warren sighed.

"True," she said. "I talked with the other Mrs. Prentiss, and she said she wished me to cooperate with you in the running of the household. She appears to have had enough of it."

"I told you so," the older woman said.

"So we can begin by touring the house," Lucy said. "And then we can take up the matter of accounts."

"Yes, Mrs. Prentiss," the housekeeper said.

The tour got under way and Lucy found herself visiting every corner of the immense lodge. They visited both corridors of the upper floor, and when they passed the room where David had his wireless outfit, she saw that the young man in the wheelchair was busy as usual. The speaker rasped out its messages and he answered by addressing the microphone on the table before him.

"Best not to disturb him," Mrs. Warren said in a whisper.

"I know," she agreed.

They continued down that corridor and

moved to the other one where she and Charles had their bedroom. She was tempted to ask the prim woman about the pearl pin, but decided against it. It would be much wiser to talk to Charles about it first and see if he could supply her with any information.

Mrs. Warren took her into another large bedroom with twin beds, and this one had its walls lined with large paintings by the late Sheila. She halted in the middle of the room and said, "This is where the master and the first lady of the house slept."

She was mildly astonished, as she thought the bedroom she was occupying with Charles had always been the master bedroom in the lodge.

She stood there in the shadowed room to ask, "Then the room we're occupying has only been made ready lately?"

"That is so," Mrs. Warren agreed. "It was a spare bedroom for guests until the news came that you and Mr. Charles had married. Then his brother had new furniture brought in and prepared it for you in a general way."

"And where do the other Mr. and Mrs. Prentiss have their room?" she asked.

"Right next to the one we're in," Mrs. Warren said. "It's almost the same size as this. I'd show it to you now, only I'd say that Mrs. Prentiss is in there."

"It doesn't matter," she said. "Let's go on."

The housekeeper next led her to a short flight of stairs off the corridor. She paused there to say, "And this leads to the attic level. There is only a storage room up there. And the studio, of course."

She gave the prim woman an inquiring glance. "You mean the studio where Sheila Prentiss did her paintings?"

"Yes."

"May I have a look at it?"

Mrs. Warren looked uneasy. She said, "I'm sorry. I don't have the key to it. After his first wife died Mr. Charles took all the keys to that room. As far as I know, he's the only one who has one. You could ask him about it."

"I will," she said. And she recalled Mabel's eerie story about Charles regularly going up to the room and locking himself in there with Sheila's paintings. As if he were trying to keep a link, slim though it might be, with the dead woman.

"There are only the cellars and the kitchen area to show you now," the gray-haired woman said rather nervously.

Lucy told her, "Then let us get on with it."

The kitchen of Seven Timbers was vast and had a flagstone floor. The cellars of the massive lodge were dank and sinister, with few improvements having been done down there since the initial building many years earlier. The only available lighting came from widely separated single bulbs set high on the rafters above them.

Mrs. Warren led the way and commented on the wine cellar, more storage areas, and what she termed Mr. Ned's room. It turned out that this was the only fully walled-off area in the cellars and that Ned Prentiss kept a collection of ancient guns there.

"The walls are lined with weapons," the prim woman said with an air of disapproval. "And naturally he doesn't let anyone but himself have the keys."

"That's probably wise," she said. "Many people have fine collections of guns."

"I think it a strange hobby," Mrs. Warren said. "Especially as Mr. Ned is a gentle man."

"I don't think it has so much to do with violence as an interest in history and inventions," she suggested.

"That could be," Mrs. Warren admitted as they reached the foot of the stairs leading to the ground floor. "Now we can go up and

84

I'll show you the house account books."

Mrs. Warren proudly led her to a small cubbyhole of a room adjoining the kitchen. There was an old-fashioned roll-top desk in it and several plain chairs — and nothing else. The single decoration on the wall was a linen towel calendar with the drawing of a red barn on it and the twelve months of the year set out in neat squares.

Lucy sat at the desk with the prim woman and went over all the various books dealing with the house accounts. Not only did she get a comprehensive view of what was required to operate the big lodge, she also saw that things had been managed very well.

As they finished, she said, "I don't think I can suggest any improvements on what you've been doing."

The eyes behind the gray-haired woman's heavy glasses showed pleasure. "Thank you, Mrs. Prentiss. I set up these records myself when I came here to work for your husband's first wife."

"Indeed," she said rising. And as an afterthought, she asked, "What was she like?"

Mrs. Warren also got to her feet and studied her in amazement. "You didn't ever know her?"

"No."

"I thought you might have," the house-keeper said. "Well, there is a self-portrait of her in the library. It was done when she was quite young, during her first year at college, I believe, so it's not too good. But it does give you an idea of her general looks."

"I'll stop by and study it," she said. "But I'm still curious as to what you felt about her."

Mrs. Warren's thin face betrayed her un-easiness. She hesitated before she said, "I liked her. There's no denying that. She had a good heart though she often lost her temper. She was no saint, but not many of us are."

"I agree," she said, listening intently, and waiting for the housekeeper to reveal more.

The prim woman frowned a little. "There were things I didn't agree with her on. Like her blaming her husband for what hap-pened to David."

"The hunting accident?"

"Yes," the housekeeper said. "That wasn't fair. And I'd be the first to admit it."

"Of course it was bound to upset her badly. She would be apt to say things she knew weren't true."

Mrs. Warren nodded. "And she did. They often quarreled about it. Right up to the last. Worst of all, it was bad for the boy. He overheard them many times, and it made him more bitter about his injury."

"He surely is bitter," she agreed. "He won't show any kind of friendship toward me."

The prim woman gave her a sympathetic look. "I'm not at all surprised. He keeps to himself too much and that wireless business is both a blessing and a curse, because it allows him to live a life independent of what goes on here."

She was struck by the housekeeper's perception in this, and said, "I think you are sadly right."

"All in all, she and Mr. Charles appeared to be as happy as most couples, except for that one quarrel about the crippling of their son. It went on and on. And perhaps in the end they were drifting apart because of it."

"That is too bad," she said. "Thank you for being so frank with me, Mrs. Warren."

"I believe in honesty," the older woman said. And then as Lucy turned to leave, she spoke out again, "There is something else you perhaps ought to know."

She stared at the gray-haired woman with the hornrimmed glasses. "Yes?"

It was evident that Mrs. Warren was

finding it difficult to select the proper words to continue. She finally said, "This is something I can only pass on to you without any personal proof."

"Please go on," she urged her.

"There have been whispers," the housekeeper said nervously, "that since the death of Sheila Prentiss this house has been haunted by her uneasy spirit."

Lucy nodded. "So I've heard."

The prim woman looked amazed. "You'd already heard about it?"

"Yes," she said. "Mrs. Mabel Prentiss told me."

"Oh?" Mrs. Warren showed bafflement.

"Though she made it seem that she was the only one who had seen the ghost. From what you say there have been others who claim the lodge is haunted."

"Yes, Mrs. Prentiss," the older woman said. "Several of the girls in the servants' quarters say they have seen a strange shadow in various parts of the building at night. A shadow that suggests the late Mrs. Prentiss to them."

"I'm not surprised," she said quietly. "As a matter of fact I have an idea I've also seen it."

"Really, madam?" Mrs. Warren sounded horrified.

"Yes. But please don't mention it. I don't want to make things worse."

"I won't," she promised, seeming badly shocked.

"It will be our secret," she said. "But if you hear anything else about the phantom being seen, I wish you'd come and tell me."

"Very well," the prim woman said.

She gave the older woman a searching look. "Why do you think Sheila's ghost might return? To try to tell us of foul play in her death?"

"I can't say," the housekeeper said in a frightened voice. "I still can't imagine how she came to fall. But I don't dare to think she was murdered."

"No," she said quietly. "Of course you wouldn't want to think that."

"This has been an unhappy place," Mrs. Warren said. "I hope your coming will change things."

"I hope so, Mrs. Warren. And thank you," she said. And with that she left the small room and the housekeeper still standing there.

She made her way toward the front of the lodge, with her mind filled with the conversation she'd had with the house-keeper. She was inclined to like the prim woman and believe the various things she had said. But there was a certain something about her that suggested that she might not be telling all she knew. A kind of nervousness that came to the surface every so often.

Halting at the library door, she went in to explore the large, book-lined room. And she let her eyes sweep around the walls, on which paintings were hung. It took her only a moment to locate the self-portrait of Sheila. It was located above the fireplace and was fairly large.

Moving over to the portrait, she gazed up at it. The face in the tempera study was pert and smilingly aggressive. Auburn hair of shoulder length framed the highly intelligent face. It was the face of someone who would be bound to love and hate strongly. A person of deep emotions!

"So you've found her!" The words were spoken in an almost jeering fashion from behind Lucy.

She wheeled around to see that it was her husband returned. He said, "I plan to remove this. I just haven't got around to it."

She gazed up at his weary, handsome face and said, "You mustn't do it on my account. After all, David is her son. He must want it here."

Charles Prentiss scowled. "What difference can it make to him? He never comes down here anyway."

She said, "I still think it should remain where it is."

"No," he said, almost too sharply. And she noticed with misgivings that all the while the discussion had been going on he had been avoiding looking at the portrait in a rather guilty fashion. And it was then, at that very moment, that a terrifying thought shot quickly across her brain. She found herself suspecting that her new husband might have had a part in the mysterious death of his first wife!

Chapter Four

The suspicion that filled her mind for a moment quickly subsided. And she saw standing facing her someone with a tortured heart rather than a murderer. A man still tormented by the loss of his wife and the mother of his son. Now he was trying himself more in an effort to please her. A needless effort!

Gently she said, "There is no need for my sake. I don't mind Sheila's portrait hanging there."

He showed astonishment. "You have every right to."

"I don't see it that way," she said. "I can't consider it of any importance. I prefer to regard it merely as a work of art. Another of her art studies. You can't clear the walls of all of them or the house would be bare, so let it remain here."

He stared at her with uncertainty. "Is that what you want?"

"Yes."

Some of his tautness seemed to leave him, though he still avoided looking at the portrait, keeping his eyes on her instead. He said, "All right. We'll let it stay there for a little, at least."

"I think that is wise," she said. "What about your cane?"

Slight annoyance tinged his handsome face. "I'm doing first rate without it."

She shook her head. "You may think so, but you could be asking for trouble. That leg isn't too strong yet."

"It's strong enough," Charles said with a bleak smile. "Let me be the judge."

"I don't want you back in the hospital," she said.

"Why not? That hospital wasn't so bad. If I hadn't gone there I would never have met you."

She laughed and said, "You're incorrigible!"

They left the library for the dining room, where Ned and his wife were already seated. Charles pulled out a chair for Lucy, and then when she was seated took his place at the head of the table.

Mabel was the first to speak, saying, "I'd like to go to Montreal tomorrow if you aren't using the plane."

Ned glanced at his brother. "What are

your plans for tomorrow?"

Charles said, "I'll be here for the balance of the week. You can have the plane. Be sure and let Ben Huggard know, or he's apt to be off hunting or on some other expedition. You know what he's like."

"I'll get in touch with him after lunch," Mabel promised.

Ned glanced across the table at Lucy and asked, "Would you like to go along? Mabel always stays overnight on her shopping trips. You might do some shopping yourself."

She hesitated, "No. I think not."

Mabel gave her husband a reproachful look. "That was a stupid suggestion, Ned. She's only just arrived here and she's trying to get used to the place. This is no time for her to leave."

"Sorry," Ned said, and gave his full attention to his food.

Charles said, "I'm inclined to agree with Mabel. It's too soon for Lucy to take a trip. Better to wait until she gets weary of being shut away here."

"I can't imagine that I will," she said with a smile for her husband. "It's so lovely. I intend to take a walk this afternoon."

"Go over through the trees on the left of the lodge," Mabel suggested. "There's a hill beyond that they use for skiing and tobogganing. You get a lovely view from there."

"Perhaps you'll come with me?" she suggested.

The blonde girl shook her head. "No thanks. I'm not all that fond of the outdoors."

Her husband raised his eyes and with a bleak smile said, "So I brought her up here where there's nothing but outdoors."

Mabel smiled at Ned. "I manage here very nicely. Just so long as I get my occasional trips to Montreal."

Charles changed the conversation by turning to his brother and telling him, "I'm going to travel up to Myles Junction this afternoon and see how the logging is going on there. We'll soon need a new supply at the mill."

"There should be plenty of logs," Ned told him. "But the main problem will be how many we can get down before spring. We count on the river to take care of most of what we cut up there."

"With things the way they are we've got to bring the stuff out by horse and sleigh and tractor team. We'll be forced to shut down the mill if we have to wait for spring delivery of the logs."

"You see what is ready and I'll work on the transportation," Ned promised him.

Charles turned to her and explained, "The world market for lumber has never been greater. So much has gone to the export trade that demand in this country isn't being met. We have dealers at us all the time for more lumber."

"How does it get to market from here?" she asked.

"By freight train," her husband said. "That's the big feature of Seven Timbers. We happen to be located directly on a main freight line, and that helps us move our product fast. But never fast enough, it seems."

"I'd like to go through the mill," Lucy said.

Charles smiled. "No problem there. I'll be glad to show you around. I can't manage it today, though, as I have to go up the line to Myles Junction."

"There's plenty of time," she said.

Ned gave her a friendly look. "I'll be in the office. Come and see me, and I'll not only take you on a tour of the mill, but I'll give you coffee and cakes when we finish."

She laughed. "That's a very tempting offer!"

"It's his standard invitation," the blonde

Mabel said with a wry smile. "You'll wind up only one of his many female visitors."

"Sounds like jealousy!" Charles teased her.

"Never!" she said. "I just want to be sure that Lucy fully understands my husband!"

"Why?" Ned asked her. "You don't."

The lovely Mabel's eyes showed anger for a moment, and then she gave him a cynical smile. "I might have expected that from you," she said. And she rose and excused herself from the table.

A few minutes later Ned also left. So she and Charles found themselves at the table alone. Charles said to her, "I often wonder how those two really get along. I get the impression there's a lot of tension just below the surface of their casual exteriors."

She shrugged. "They bicker. Many husbands and wives do, without it meaning anything."

Charles gazed at her earnestly. "I hope we don't ever fall into the habit. I dislike it intensely."

"I'll remember," she said.

He finished his coffee and touched his napkin to his lips. "I'm sorry I have to leave you this afternoon, but I want to get away and back before it's dark."

"I understand."

"I'm glad you're interested in the mill," he said.

"I am."

"Mabel doesn't have any interest in it at all."

"Then why did she marry your brother?"

Charles grimaced. "That oughtn't to be hard to guess. She was interested in his money."

"You think that's all?"

"That's about it," her husband said as he rose to help her up from the table. "I'd just as soon not think about it."

She was struck by his sudden bitterness, and so said nothing more on the subject. Charles and she went out to the living room, and he was standing there about to get his coat and hat and leave when she suddenly remembered the pearl pin she'd so mysteriously found in her jewel case. The pin that had belonged to Sheila.

She said, "Before you go I have something to ask you."

"Yes?" he waited to see what it might be.

She reached in her pocket and produced the pearl pin and asked, "Have you seen this before?"

He stared at it incredulously and took it in his hands to examine it. Then, looking up from it, he demanded, "Where did you get this?"

"In my jewel case. It belonged to Sheila, didn't it?"

"Yes," he said, gazing at the pin again. "It did."

"I thought you might have left it for me."

Hearing this, his manner changed at once. And in what was a plainly upset state he told her, "I found it and put it there for you. I'm glad you've gotten it safely!"

"Mabel said it was lost. That you couldn't find it," she told him.

His handsome face drained of color. "Yes, it was lost," he said nervously.

"But you found it?"

He nodded. "Yes. I found it. And now you have it, which is what I wanted." He gave the pin to her.

Taking it, she said, "It's lovely! Thank you!"

"I thought you would enjoy it," he said, and rather hastily took her in his arms and kissed her. "I must go," he told her. "Otherwise I won't get back until late."

He hurried out of the living room, leaving her standing there with the fabulous pearl pin in her hand. And she found herself not believing him. It seemed to her that he had been shocked to find the pin in

99

her possession. He had quickly made up the story of leaving it for her in her jewel case. Why? It was another of the many mysteries that she'd encountered in the sinister lodge!

But if his story weren't true and he hadn't left the pin for her, how had it found its way to her jewel case? This made an even greater mystery and seemed to bolster the theory that the old mansion was the habitat of a ghost. The ghost of Sheila! She glanced at the pin again and a tiny shudder ran down her spine.

She made her way up the left stairway and went down the corridor toward her room when Mabel suddenly appeared to block her way.

The Nordic, blonde Mabel smiled at her knowingly. "Did you ask Charles about the pin?"

"Yes."

"What did he say?"

Feeling that she might be guilty of disloyalty to Charles and yet not wanting to lie about it, she said uneasily, "He claimed he found the pin and placed it in the jewel box for me to find."

Mabel gave a taut little laugh. She said, "I thought he would come up with something like that."

"You did?" She wondered if Mabel was just playing wise.

"Of course. He had to give you an explanation. He wouldn't want you to start believing in the ghost."

Shocked, she said, "Why not?"

"Think about it," was all that Mabel would say. And with that the blonde girl in the chic blue gown vanished back into her own room.

She stared at the closed door with dismay. Mabel was clearly trying to cause trouble between her and Charles. All this talk about the pin couldn't be put down to helpfulness on her part. She wanted to create dissension and this was one of the ways she planned to do it.

Lucy continued on to the bedroom she shared with Charles with her mind troubled by all that had happened. She even wondered if Mabel might have gone out to the balcony overlooking the living room and eavesdropped on the conversation she'd had with Charles. She was slowly coming to the conclusion that the blonde girl was angry at losing the dominant role in the household and so had decided to make things as unpleasant for her as possible.

On the other hand it could be that her

sister-in-law was trying to warn her about something, trying to make her understand something that she dared not suggest directly. And again the dark shadow of Charles possibly being responsible for Sheila's death came to trouble her.

She opened her jewel case and carefully placed the pearl pin in it. Then she put the case away and set about dressing for her planned walk. She wanted to go out before the strength of the midday sun weakened too greatly. She put on her skiing clothes, including a woolly hood, which she buttoned under her chin to give her ears better protection.

Then she quickly made her way back to the balcony and down the right stairway. As she hurried down its extremely steep incline she suddenly remembered that it was down these very stairs that Sheila had plunged to her death. She at once slackened her pace and took a stiffer grip on the railing.

As she reached the living room, Mrs. Warren appeared from the dining-room doorway. The prim woman smiled at her. "You look pretty and so young in that outfit, Mrs. Prentiss."

"Thank you," she said. "I bought it for skiing but I haven't used it much."

102

"You can use clothes like that up here," the housekeeper assured her. "In fact I don't know what you'd do without them."

"I'm glad I came prepared," she smiled.

Mrs. Warren continued to stare at her. "You do look young, Mrs. Prentiss. And I just heard from cook that you were a widow before you married Mr. Charles. Now I find that hard to believe."

"Oh? Well, it's true." She was intrigued that she had already become a subject of conversation below stairs.

"You lived in the South, didn't you?"

"Yes. In South Carolina," she said. "But I had relatives in Maine, and that is what brought me back."

"Well, I never!" Mrs. Warren said. "It's a strange world! But I mustn't keep you here in your warm clothes!"

Lucy was glad to get away from the housekeeper and out of the great lodge. She had found Mrs. Warren talkative, and this had worked out to her advantage most of the time. But just now it had been a nuisance. She was amazed that the servants had found out so much information about her. No doubt one of them had heard about her and passed the news on. She couldn't imagine how it had reached them otherwise.

Standing on the verandah of the lodge she adjusted to the cold air. And she decided that she was dressed warmly enough for her proposed walk. She went down the verandah steps and across the path that cut over the snow-covered lawn. She had to stay with the path, as the snow was almost three feet high on the level and even higher in places where it had drifted.

After she'd gone a little way she halted and turned to stare back at the sprawling lodge on the hill. Its log walls, covered with icicles, gleamed in the sunlight. It was not a good-looking building but it had a certain majesty. Its huge bulk, entirely constructed of logs, was different and impressive. It was her first glimpse of it in daylight, and she studied it for quite a few moments.

Then she walked on in the direction of the row of tall fir and spruce trees that Mabel had told her shielded the hillside and the ski run from the old mansion. To the right were the village and the mills. The mills were big gray buildings and there were enclosed walks joining some of the structures at a level high above the ground. She assumed these walks allowed workers to move from one building to another without going out into the cold.

The sun was still relatively strong but the air was frigid. Her breath showed in it as she walked along. Gradually she neared the evergreens, which at close range seemed taller than she'd imagined. She followed the path, on its way through this minor forest. The trees were mantled with snow, and large icicles hung from many of the branches.

She continued on and now she missed the full benefits of the sun, as it shone through only at occasional places. For no reason she could understand she suddenly felt isolated and fearful. Perhaps it was the silence and immensity of the forest in this white-clad country. She couldn't be sure. But a sense of alarm coursed through her and she began to walk a little faster, anxious to emerge from the shadowed forest.

Without warning she heard a sound that seemed to come from behind and perhaps above her. She cried out in fear at the same moment that something struck her a resounding blow on the back of the head and sent her falling face forward into the snow in an unconscious state.

Her first awareness was of someone turning her over, and then she stared up with glazed eyes and saw that another face was looking down into hers. It took her a moment to focus her vision and see that it was the pilot, Ben Huggard.

He said, "You got a nasty clout on the head."

"I know," she said faintly.

"Lucky you were wearing that woolly hat," he told her.

Her mind was now beginning to work normally, and she at once sat up, aware that her head was aching. She asked, "What happened?"

"Winter accident," he said. "One of the heavy icicles dropped from a tree branch and hit you. These woods can be dangerous."

"An icicle!" she gasped, unable to believe this was what had happened.

"Sure," he said in his mocking way. He picked up a fragment of heavy, broken icicle from beside her for her to see, then he tossed it away. "That ice is like iron!"

"I've a terrible headache," she said, but at the same time she struggled to her feet.

He quickly came to her aid and held her for a moment after she was standing. "All right? Not going to faint or anything?"

"No."

The pilot grinned at her. And again she was aware of his arrogance as he said, "You've got a lot of courage."

"Thanks," she said. "But I seem to be

light on good sense. I never dreamed of there being any danger from falling ice."

"You always remember that in winter," Ben Huggard told her. "People have been killed in the middle of the largest cities from ice falling from buildings and cracking their skulls. Out here we have to be careful of high places and trees."

"I'll remember that," she said ruefully.

"It's worse at this time of day," he said. "The sun has been up long enough to weaken the ice."

"I see," she said, her head still aching but not as much as before.

"At night you'd be safe, or in the early morning."

"I'll remember that and walk through woods only in the early morning," she said.

"Want to take off that hat for a moment and see if the skin on your skull is broken?" the pilot asked.

"Should I?"

"I think so," Ben Huggard said.

"All right," she sighed, and she took off the hat, baring her head for him. "It's freezing! Don't take long to look!"

"I won't," he said as he quickly parted the hair and found the injured spot.

"Hurts when you touch it!" she exclaimed.

"Quite an egg up there but no skin broken," he said cheerily. "Put your hat back on and rub some decent liniment on it when you get back to the lodge."

She pulled on her hat and buttoned it under her chin. "I could have saved myself that trouble!"

Ben Huggard's round face showed another of his grins. "That's the thanks I get for offering first-aid!" He was wearing what looked like riding breeches and high-laced boots, plus a red jacket and a red-and-white checked woolen cap.

She said, "What were you doing out here?"

"On my way to the ski run. I often cross through the woods."

"Were you going skiing?"

"No," he said. "I just wanted to see if there were any of my buddies there. There's a tavern in the village where I go with some of them on afternoons when I'm not working."

"I see," she said.

"Can I walk you back home?" he asked.

"I think not," she said. "Since I've come this far, I may as well go the rest of the way. I'll continue on to the ski run."

The tall, round-faced pilot seemed amused by this. "I said you had courage," he told her. "And since you've made up your mind, I'll go along with you."

"Thanks," she said.

"You're not taking me out of my way," he assured her.

They began walking on through the woods. Her head still ached with every step she took, but she felt she'd been lucky enough to escape without any serious injury. She knew she should be grateful to the man at her side for coming to her aid, but somehow she didn't feel properly about it. She was ashamed that she was allowing her personal dislike for him to stop her from appreciating what he'd done for her.

His arrogance upset her. It seemed that he continually had a chip on his shoulder. That while he worked as a fairly menial employee for her husband and his brother, he liked to think of himself as equal or even above them in intelligence. Perhaps this was so, she thought crossly, but if it were the case, why didn't he strike out and make a name for himself somewhere else rather than continuing on as a pilot at Seven Timbers?

He said, "You're a lot different from the first Mrs. Charles Prentiss."

"Really?" She thought this another example of his arrogance.

"You bet," the pilot said. "She was a looker but she had a rotten disposition. Everyone was dirt to her."

"I don't know anything about her," she said, wishing that she were alone or that she'd decided to go back to the lodge.

Ben gave her a glance. "You're different. You know how to get along with people."

"I hope so," she said.

"That Mabel is another one!" he said with disgust. "Wants to go to Montreal tomorrow. Leaves me at the airport and doesn't even say thank you. Just tells me the time to be there waiting for her the next morning. I guess her husband might be surprised if he knew where she went at night. You can bet there's a man mixed up in those trips she takes!"

She gave him a warning look. "You oughtn't to talk like that."

He shrugged. "I know you won't repeat what I said."

"I'd rather not hear it!"

Ben Huggard laughed nastily. "The sooner you know what goes on at Seven Timbers the better off you'll be! And I'm just the lad to tell you."

"I'm sure you are," she said, "but I don't want to hear it from you. Let me find out for myself."

"You will," he said in his jeering fashion. Then he suddenly halted and looked back. In a taut voice he said, "There's someone following us."

"Following us? Don't you mean walking through the woods?"

"Same thing," the tall man said, still staring back. She gazed up at him with an expression of disbelief on her pretty face. "This is a public path. Anyone has a right to walk on it."

Ben Huggard was paying no attention to her. He whistled to himself. "It's John Rhode!" he exclaimed. "I wonder how long he's been trailing us!"

"Does it matter?"

Ben gave her a startled look. "No. I guess not. It just gave me a start. This is a lonely country up here."

"I thought you knew everyone and everyone knew you," she said with derision in her tone. She couldn't resist it.

Ben Huggard turned and said, "We might as well walk on."

"Why not wait for John Rhode?"

He gave her an ugly look, "You know him?"

"Of course. He came and picked us up at the plane last night. Surely you remember."

"I didn't for a minute," he said. "He's

not so much. Has a share in the mills but he lets your husband and Ned do all the work."

"I'm not too interested in that," she said.

"He's always nosing around prying into other people's business," the pilot went on complaining. "Thinks he's the unofficial mayor or something!"

By this time the maligned John Rhode was coming close to them. He was wearing a ski outfit in dark blue and look rather good in it.

He greeted her first with a smile. "You're a long way from the lodge," he said.

"I decided to take a walk. Mabel told me about a ski run on the other side of the woods."

"You're almost there," John Rhode told her. And he turned to the pilot and said, "Hello, Ben."

"Hello," Ben said without enthusiasm.

She was quick to tell John Rhode, "We met here in the woods."

"Did you?" John Rhode said with a knowing look on his gaunt, intelligent face.

"I had an accident." And she told him about it.

"I find that unusual," John Rhode said. "I've never heard of such an accident in these woods."

"You're wrong," Ben said harshly. "Icicles fall and hit people all the time."

The gaunt-faced John Rhode said, "That may be your experience, but I can promise you it hasn't been mine." There was a marked contrast between the two young men. John Rhode was all quiet assurance and aristocratic in bearing, while the larger Ben Huggard was arrogant, mocking, and obviously of limited background.

She thought she should try to stop any argument about her mishap, so she said, "I guess we ought to all walk on to the ski run."

"Why not?" John Rhode asked pleasantly as he strolled along at her side. "Have you had time enough yet to decide how you feel about Seven Timbers?"

"Not really," she said. "But somehow I think I'm going to adjust to it very well."

"I hope so," John Rhode said.

Ben Huggard was lumbering along a little ahead of them with a scowl on his round face. It was evident that he didn't care for John Rhode and resented him intruding on them. Lucy found this amusing, as it was exactly what she'd wanted.

They reached the edge of the woods, and she saw the ski run and the valley below. In the distance there was another high ridge of mountains. It was a magnificent sight, worth taking the time and effort to see.

"What a lovely view!" she enthused.

Ben Huggard was scanning the slope bleakly. "No one here at all," he said. "They must have decided not to ski today."

She asked him, "So what will you do now?"

"Go on to the village," the pilot said. "But not back through the woods. I'll go down the slope and use a shortcut."

"I see," she said. "Well, thanks for coming to my aid."

Some of the old mockery returned to his manner as he said airily, "Any time." And with that he left them and started trudging down the slope and heading left in the direction of the village. She and John Rhode stood at the top of the ski run and watched his retreating figure.

John broke the silence by saying, "I have an idea he objected to my joining you."

"I can't imagine why," she protested. "I didn't start out with him. He came along after my accident."

"So I gathered," John Rhode said dryly. "Well, you can't be blamed for that."

She smiled ruefully. "The truth is I don't like him. He makes me terribly nervous.

He always has such a chip on his shoulder."

John Rhode eyed her with interest. "You've noticed that?"

"How can you help it?"

"Some people seem to miss it."

"I can't think why," she exclaimed. "He has arrogance written all over him."

"I fully agree," John Rhode said. "But he has a rough charm, and he happens to be a good pilot."

"So my husband and Ned keep him on?"

"Yes," the gaunt-faced man agreed. He gave her a wise look. "I don't mind telling you now I was a little worried for you when I saw you together."

"You thought he'd made another conquest?"

"Not entirely that," the man at her side said carefully. "I was more afraid of your being alone in his company. And I'm not sure about that story of your being struck by an icicle."

This startled her. She stared at him, "Meaning what?"

"I don't care to speculate too much about it," he said. "I'm just saying the story sounds thin to me."

"But I was knocked out by the falling ice!"

"You were knocked out," John Rhode

corrected her. "Whether it was from falling ice or not has to be proven. You didn't see the ice as it hit you, did you?"

"No."

"You were struck down without really knowing what it was that did it?"

"You're right," she said, a strange expression crossing her face. "I have only his word for it."

"That's what I mean," John Rhode said. "So let us think about it for a while longer."

She was intrigued and shocked by what he said. Considering his words, she gathered that Ben Huggard might not be adverse to attacking a single woman alone in the woods. Of course he hadn't said anything openly, but there was a good deal implied in his manner.

She said, "Well, I've seen the slope and valley, now I must go back."

"I'll see you safely on your way," John Rhode suggested.

She shook her head. "No. You came here to ski. I don't want to spoil your afternoon."

His gaunt, yet pleasant face showed a warm smile. "I ought to have been working anyway. I played hookey from the mill this afternoon."

She smiled. "You probably aren't all that busy, are you?"

"I could find plenty to do," he said. "I'm in sales in the main office. But I prefer to work an occasional night and then take a day or even an afternoon off when I like."

"It sounds logical," she said.

"It suits me," he told her. "Now we'll start the return trip through the woods."

She gave him a worried glance. "I'm sure I'd do all right on my own. I don't want to take you all the way back."

The thin man smiled. "Not even if I find your company more exciting than the prospect of skiing alone for an hour?"

Lucy blushed. "That's a very nice compliment."

"And sincerely offered," he said, taking her by the arm. "Let's go."

So they started back along the path through the tall, snow-mantled trees. And now the sun was less strong than before, so the path was shaded and bitterly cold. She knew that she was deeply grateful for the gaunt young man's company, though she did not want to make him uncomfortable by repeating it over and over.

As they walked, he said, "You know that Sheila and I were sister and brother?"

"Yes. Charles told me."

"I'm glad," the man at her side said with a tiny frown. "And I don't want you to think I'm against you because as the wife of Charles you are taking Sheila's place."

"That is something I have never aspired to," she said. "I only want to make Charles as happy as I can in my own right."

"Nicely said," John Rhode commented with approval. "Naturally I was shaken by my sister's tragic death."

"You would be bound to be," she sympathized.

"But I have no objection to Charles marrying again."

"Of course you wouldn't have," she agreed.

He gave her a sharp glance as he went on to say, "But what might bother me would be if his second wife also had a mysterious accident."

Chapter Five

The fact that the young man's quiet statement was so completely unexpected filled her with a double sense of shock. She halted and stared at him, thinking that he could only be insinuating that Charles might have had something to do with Sheila's death. And that because of this her own position was far from secure. She had thought this briefly on her own, but she'd not expected her troubled imaginings to be confirmed by someone else.

She said, "You're not satisfied about Sheila's death?"

"I'm not satisfied with anything," he said evasively. "And I'd be very upset if you should die from, some accident — say from a bit of falling ice from a tree. I'll be truthful, it would make me suspicious."

Her eyes widened in panic. "Of Charles?"

"Of someone," he said. "But you weren't hurt badly, so there is nothing to be concerned about, is there?"

"I suppose not," she said doubtfully.

"At least not for the moment," he said in a significant manner as they started to walk on again.

She admitted, "I have been puzzled by the facts of your sister's death. There is a great deal of mystery about that night."

"I know."

"And yet it may have been a true accident."

"It well could have been," he agreed.

She said, "I feel I'm being unfaithful to Charles when I allow myself to have such suspicions. I've felt this way only since I've arrived here. Perhaps it is the old house and the bleakness of the surroundings. You begin to imagine things."

"We can be influenced by our surroundings," said the gaunt young man walking beside her along the path through the snowy woods.

"I want to be fair with Charles. He suffered a great deal in losing Sheila. Then he had that dreadful accident."

"That was strange too," John Rhode observed. "Charles is always very careful in the mills. I don't know what happened that day."

"Nor does he," she said.

He gave her a glance. "You've talked to him about it?"

"As much as I was able to. He didn't seem anxious to discuss it."

"I'm not surprised."

"Why?"

John Rhode shrugged. "One doesn't try to explain what one doesn't understand."

"I see," she said. "I believe Mabel was there at the time, but she hasn't spoken about it."

"Mabel would not be a reliable witness," he said.

"You think not?"

"No. She's given to hysterics in a crisis. She had a spell as soon as she learned of Sheila's accidental death. It was rather shocking."

"I didn't hear about that."

"Probably not," the young man said bleakly. "Since I've said so much I may as well tell you something else. But I want your word you won't repeat it."

"Anything you tell me in confidence I'll respect," she said.

"I hope so," he sighed. "I don't want any trouble with your husband."

They had emerged from the forest of evergreens now and were standing in the open snow-covered field. Not far ahead of them loomed the log majesty of Seven Timbers. She stared at the young man beside her, puzzled by his words.

She said, "What is it you have to tell me?"

He met her eyes directly. "Before my sister's death there was a good deal of gossip in the village about Charles and a girl who worked in our office."

"Charles and a girl!" she said in utter shock.

He nodded gravely. "I knew the girl. She had a desk not far from mine. She was attractive, and she and Charles worked a lot together and appeared to get along well. Some people felt too well."

"And?"

"Sheila heard about it and questioned me on the subject. I told her I thought there was nothing to it. I would have told her that anyway, since I wouldn't want to make her unhappy."

"Was there anything to it?"

"I think not," he said. "But I don't know. I guess no one ever will. Right after the accident that sent Charles to the hospital, the girl gave up her job here and left. She gave no forwarding address, and no one has heard of her since."

"That seems very strange," Lucy said.

"Charles asking you to marry him and bringing you back as his bride strikes me as even more strange," John Rhode said. "I don't see him doing that if there had been anything to the affair. He could have had no knowledge of her leaving. And I doubt if he would have tried to bring back a wife if he'd had a mistress here. This is a small town."

Listening to his explanation made her feel better. She was sure that he was right and that Charles must be innocent. She said, "I agree."

He studied her soberly. "You're probably wondering why I have told you this."

"I am," she said.

"I thought it better that you hear it from me first," he said. "At least I'm trying to give you a fair picture of what went on. You would be almost certain to get bits and pieces from some of the others in the village with the facts distorted."

"I see."

"You are in Sheila's shoes now, so to speak," he went on. "I wasn't able to save her life, but I would like to be of some help to you."

She said, "You make it sound as if my life could be in danger!"

"Who knows?" he said. "Maybe it is."

"I can't think why!" she protested.

John Rhode smiled thinly. "I'm glad your mind is at ease. I hope it remains so. That nothing happens to disturb it. And I trust that your marriage to Charles is a happy one."

"Thank you," she said with some irony as she considered his many revelations to her.

"You may think I have done my best to spoil your bliss," he went on. "Not so. I merely wish to have you in possession of all the facts. Then you can think things out for yourself."

"Thanks."

"One other thing, and I won't keep you standing here in the cold," he apologized. "I wish you'd try and help my nephew, David."

"I've already tried. It isn't going to be easy. He seems to have a hatred for everyone. All that interests him is his wireless set."

"Sheila was able to reach him."

"She was his mother."

"Granted," the gaunt-faced young man agreed. "But I still wish you'd try. He needs sympathy and help."

"I will," she said.

"Good," John Rhode said, sounding

pleased as they resumed their walk to the entrance of Seven Timbers. "I've been very honest with you. A lot of what I've said will be best kept to yourself."

"I understand."

"And you needn't feel guilty about it. Charles has not been a saint. You mustn't think of him as being above the normal. I'm saying this for your protection."

"I'll be discreet," she promised.

"Do you ski?" he asked, abruptly changing the subject.

"Not well."

"Neither do I," he said. "But I enjoy it. Will you come out with me some afternoon?"

"All right," she said.

He confided in her, "Since Sheila's death I've not visited Seven Timbers often. I found it too painful. But from now on I'll be open to accept dinner invitations if you wish to offer them."

"I will invite you," she promised. "I want to talk to you some more."

John Rhode smiled at her as they reached the verandah steps. "And I would like to be your friend."

"I need one here badly."

"You have one," he assured her. "You can reach me by telephone at any hour of the day or night. If you have any reason to think you're in trouble, don't hesitate to call on me."

"I won't," she promised. "Would you like to come in and have a drink?"

"Not now, thank you," he said.

"Another time then."

"Yes. Another time."

They parted and she went inside and up to the bedroom. Her mind was whirling with all that John Rhode had told her. It seemed that her new husband was a much more complex man than she'd give him credit for. The suggestion that he'd been carrying on an affair with a girl in the office at the time of his wife's mysterious death also was something to think about. Again it brought forth the possibility that Charles might have been in some way associated with Sheila's accident.

She stared ruefully at herself in the dresser mirror as she removed her warm outer clothing. She'd only been at Seven Timbers a few days and she was already suspecting her husband of being a murderer! It was both contemptible and ridiculous of her! She hated herself for it.

And yet there were these rumors and odd happenings that would make anyone suspicious. She could understand that

John Rhode might be prejudiced against her husband, since he was Sheila's brother. But she also felt that the gaunt, cultured young man was a most honest person. So what to believe remained an enigma.

She must try and view things objectively. Take a mild line and give Charles the benefit of any doubts. She owed that to him as his wife. The supposed affair with the girl in the office might have been an innocent thing enlarged by gossip to stupid proportions. The very fact that the girl had left the village during the time Charles was in the hospital seemed to suggest that it had been no more than a friendship.

Going into the bathroom she searched until she found a suitable liniment and applied it to the bump on her head. She recalled that John Rhodes had been cynical about Ben Huggard's version of how the bump had occurred. And she wondered what might really have happened, if she'd not been given the truth by the pilot. Had she been struck down by someone using the icicle as a weapon? Had Ben then come upon her and, seeing the icicle by her head, decided it had fallen on her?

She knew it was a possibility, but she preferred the more simple explanation that the icicle had fallen from a tree branch.

Returning to the bedroom she spent a few minutes rearranging her hair. She was now thinking about the arrogant Ben and the way he'd acted when John Rhodes had showed up. There was certainly no love lost between the two men.

Ben had maintained his mocking, superior air toward her. And he'd even gone so far as to accuse Mabel of having a lover whom she met on her shopping expeditions to Montreal. He had taken a chance in making such a statement. She knew if she went to Charles or Ned and told them it would likely cost Ben Huggard his pilot's job. But what if his story were true? Would anything be accomplished by passing it on? Not likely.

The beautiful Mabel struck her as being a devious person. And she could tell that the marriage between the blonde and the serious Ned was not an ideal one. She didn't want to be mixed up in any quarrels they might have, and so she would say nothing. But Ben had started her thinking, and from now on she would watch for any signs that what he said about Mabel might be true.

John Rhode had made a special point of asking her to be friendly to young David. She wanted to do what she could for the

128

seventeen-year-old youth, but he insisted on showing only coldness toward her. Yet, if only for his sake, she would keep on trying to win his favor.

With a sigh she left the bedroom and went down the corridor to the balcony and then along the other corridor to David's room. When she drew near it she heard the usual rasping from the loudspeaker of the wireless set.

A voice was calling, "DP 606! Are you there? DP 606, this is MIZ 32 in Buffalo calling."

She walked on toward the door, and just as she approached it she was surprised to hear the set suddenly snapped off. When she reached the doorway the wireless set was dead and the tiny room was enjoying an unusual silence. As for David, he sat slumped in his wheelchair glaring at the bank of wireless apparatus.

Lucy went on in and said, "Hello!"

The youth in the chair, whose features were so like those of his handsome father, turned to glance at her in his regular sullen fashion.

"What do you want?" he asked.

She smiled. "I mainly wanted to come by and see you?"

"Why?"

She shrugged. "I'd like us to be friends. I thought you might explain something about the workings of your wireless set."

David scowled. "I don't want to talk about it. I'm fed up to the ears with it!"

Her eyes widened in surprise. "You are tired of it?"

"Wouldn't you be if you stayed up here day after day and had nothing else to occupy you?" he demanded with some anger in his voice.

She leaned against the table as she talked with him. "Haven't you deliberately made a prisoner of yourself?"

"I had to do something to be independent of the others."

"Is that so important?" she asked quietly.

The golden-haired youth shifted in his compact wheelchair. "It is to me."

"None of us are ever entirely self-sufficient."

"You're not a cripple!" he challenged her.

"That's true," she said. "And I don't mean to sound as if I were preaching. I haven't the right. But I've learned the best thing to do when we're faced with a loss of any sort is to try and make up for it some way."

David eyed her with a shadow of sarcasm on his handsome face. "You sound as if you've had a lot of experience. I don't see you suffering from anything."

"Suffering isn't always visible," she said. "I lost my husband. I had to begin over again and make an entire new way of life. And I managed to do it by returning to nursing. And it was through that I met your father."

The youth in the wheelchair showed surprise. "I didn't know you were a widow. What happened to your husband?"

The mere fact that he was showing some interest in her and was willing to talk was a gain. She said, "He died very suddenly of a brain tumor. I wasn't prepared for it. It was a bad blow for me."

"My mother died suddenly. You know about her fall?"

"Yes."

His face became troubled. "If I hadn't been so occupied with this wireless I might have heard her and gotten to her in time to save her life."

"From what I heard she must have died at once."

"They don't really know."

Changing the subject, she said, "Before your accident you must have been active."

"I was."

131

"And now you don't try to get out of that chair?"

He gave her a wary look. "No."

"Why not? Your father says you had some therapy and you were able to get around with crutches."

"I hate crutches."

"Oh?" She saw his resentment flaring up again and knew she must be careful or all the good she'd managed in making a contact with him would be lost.

He scowled. "Father wants to see me limping around on crutches so he can tell himself I'm getting better. He doesn't want to face up to the truth — that because of him I'm crippled for life."

"Because of him?"

"He took me hunting with him that day!"

She said, "Wasn't that only because he enjoyed your company?"

"He should have told me about the gun. Warned me it was that easy to go off. I thought the safety catch was working right, and he knew it wasn't but he didn't warn me!"

Lucy imagined she could hear the unhappy Sheila going over this time and again. Drilling this grim thought into her own mind and that of her son. Accusing her husband of criminal carelessness!

Quietly she said, "We all are liable to make mistakes. It could be that your father omitted warning you about the faulty catch through forgetfulness. I agree it was terribly unfortunate, but can you go on hating because of a moment of faulty memory on your father's part? An error that you or I or anyone might make?"

His reaction was strange. It was as if the thought had never been presented to him this way before. Stubbornly he maintained, "He had no right to forget."

"It isn't a matter of having a right," she corrected him. "It's a matter of human error, and we're all prone to it."

David hesitated and then said, "You are bound to stick up for him, since you're his wife!"

"Only if I think he's in the right," she said.

"So you're telling me I'm in the wrong! That I crippled myself!"

"Of course not," she said. "I think what happened to you was an unfortunate accident. But blaming your father isn't going to help. Only trying to surmount what happened to you will do that. I think you've tried to bury yourself in this wireless, and while it must have been helpful to you for a time, I don't think you should tie yourself to this bench and your call letters. Try to lead a life with larger dimensions."

"In a wheelchair?"

"It's been done," she said. "And forgive me for getting on the platform again. I've talked too much."

David looked cynical. "At least you have enough sense to know that."

"I'm not really all that stupid or self-seeking," she said.

The youth in the wheelchair crimsoned. "Did I say you were?"

"I think you believe it," she said quietly. "I'd like you to understand that while I married your father in the hope of furthering my own happiness, it is also important to me that I further his. And if I'm to do that I must somehow be your friend. Think it over."

She left him sitting in the chair staring after her in complete surprise. She knew that to remain a moment longer would risk spoiling any progress she'd made with the youth, and she wasn't convinced she'd made any. He was fiercely loyal to his dead mother, and she understood that.

As she walked up the corridor toward the balcony she heard him turn the wireless set on again, and the rasping of call letters started over the loudspeaker once more. She couldn't help worrying about David's future and wondering what might eventually happen to him.

She halted on the balcony and looked down to see the beautiful, blonde Mabel seated in an easy chair before the fireplace reading a magazine. Mabel apparently sensed her presence on the balcony, as she looked up at her and placed the magazine aside.

"Come down and talk for a moment," the blonde invited her.

"I didn't see you when I came in," she said, descending the left stairway.

"I was in my room."

"Oh."

"I saw you coming back to the house with John Rhode," Mabel said. "Did you enjoy your walk?"

She seated herself in a chair across from the other girl. "To a point," she said.

"How did you come to meet John?" The blonde was curious about this.

She at once went into a recital of her experience in the woods, including Ben Huggard's coming to her rescue, and John Rhode joining them. She finished by saying, "After Ben left us John offered to see me back safely."

Mabel said, "That was a strange sort of accident."

"Ben claims it happens fairly often."

"That's true," the blonde woman agreed. "I was almost hit by a falling icicle just outside the house once."

"I'll be careful in the future," she said ruefully.

"Ben would enjoy playing the hero," Mabel said with a sour smile.

"I find him very strange."

"Do you?"

"Yes," she said. "He's so terribly over-bearing."

"I know," Mabel said. "He hates the Prentiss family. There is a surprising percentage of the people here in the village who do."

"Then why do they stay here?"

The blonde girl shrugged. "I guess they're afraid to leave and strike out for themselves. They'd rather complain about us as the oppressors and go on working for us."

"Ben continually makes me uncomfortable," she said.

"It doesn't mean anything. He left here for a time and then came back to be the company pilot. It's a good, easy job, and he stays here because he knows he can't do better anywhere else."

"But if he hates us it can't be all that pleasant for him."

"Some people enjoy hating," Mabel said. "I can tell you another one — John Rhode."

Her eyebrows rose in surprise. "I can't think that! He's so nice. And he's a man of culture."

"But he hates Charles and Ned," Mabel warned her. "He is linked with our husbands in business, but I think he'd do anything to harm them that he dared."

"Why?"

"The Prentiss mill swallowed up his father's business and left him with only an unimportant job and a small share of the company. And Sheila married Charles — and you know how that turned out."

She admitted, "I sensed he was a little bitter about that."

Mabel said, "He's never been in this house since Sheila's death."

"He told me that," she said. "And he promised that if he were invited now he'd come."

"Because you're here?"

She blushed. "I don't know."

"Of course it's that," Mabel declared. "He has no use for the rest of us."

137

"He is concerned about David."

Mabel rolled her blue eyes. "Naturally! David is his blood relation. He'd dote on him because he's Sheila's son."

"There's nothing wrong in that," she said.

"Not if it isn't pushed too far. But I'm sure John Rhode would take up where Sheila left off in trying to make David hate his father."

"Do you really believe that?" she asked with some concern. "I see John Rhode as being a fair man."

Mabel's lip curled in a derisive smile. "I can tell you're one of those people who goes around seeing good in everyone. I warn you that can be fatal."

"So can seeing evil in everyone."

"It's a lot more realistic," Mabel told her as she picked up her magazine again. "Do you know I think the skirts are getting long again? I can't wait to get to Montreal tomorrow and do some shopping."

"It bothers you up here."

"It does," the blonde said. "I live only to get away."

"Perhaps if you explained to Ned, he'd find a plan to live in a larger city like Montreal."

Mabel gave a mock groan. "I've done

nothing but try and persuade him to move to the city. It has done no good at all. He just doesn't listen to me! His only interests are up here!"

Because she found the blonde young woman in a nervous and rather bitter mood, she didn't remain too long with her. Instead she went back up to her bedroom and had a short sleep during the late afternoon. She had just risen from the bed and begun to freshen herself for dinner when her husband entered the bedroom. A single glance at him caused her concern. His face had a taut look of pain.

She went over to him at once. "Is anything wrong?"

"Not really," he said, even his voice tense. "I stumbled when I was up in the woods and strained my bad leg a little."

"What did I tell you about your cane?" she reminded him.

His smile was grim. "You were right," he agreed. "Well, now I'm paying the price."

"Sit down," she said, urging him over to a chair.

He sat without too much resistance, and glancing up at her said, "I think I'll take a warm tub before dinner."

"It might help," she agreed. "You sit there and I'll draw the water for you."

"No need," he protested.

"I'm glad to do it. And the less you move around the better. Tomorrow you must use your cane, and take the weight off that leg until it has a chance to recuperate."

"I will," he promised.

"You say that," she sighed. "I never know whether you mean it or not."

"I do," he insisted. "How did your day go?"

"I'll tell you after I have your bath water under way," she said. And she hurried into the bathroom and turned on the hot and cold water taps. When she had them properly adjusted to offer a warm tub, she went back to join her husband. And she told him about the afternoon's events.

He frowned as she finished and said, "Don't go into the woods again alone."

"I'm not liable to," she said wryly.

"This is a remote country," he said. "There are often wild animals roaming out there. I don't say they'd harm you, but there is always a chance."

"I know."

"And about John Rhode," Charles said with a deep sigh. "I can only advise that you don't become too friendly with him."

"Why?"

"I feel he is my enemy," Charles said in

much the same spirit in which Mabel had spoken. "He can't forgive me for Sheila's death, or David's accident for that matter."

"Are you sure you aren't imagining that?"

Charles gave her a sharp look of rebuke. "Give me credit for knowing something about people who have been around me for years. John avoids me now. At the office it is very difficult. If he weren't a partner I would dismiss him."

"He said he'd like to come to dinner."

Charles showed shock. "He told you that?"

"Yes."

Her husband grimly compressed his lips. "Then he has to be up to something. Perhaps he wants to try to turn you against me."

She said, "Why should anyone want to do that?"

Charles' handsome face had a tragic expression on it. "He knows that my life has been devastated by the tragedies here. Probably he sees that you might make living bearable for me again and he wants to deny me that."

"I can't think that anyone would be so deliberately evil," she protested.

"Wait and see," her husband said.

"Better go in and take your warm tub," she told him. "The water will be cold if you don't."

"Very well," he said, getting up from the chair with difficulty. He limped over to the bathroom and went in and closed the door.

She waited for him in the bedroom, not wanting to go down and join Ned and his wife until Charles was with her. She stared out at the growing darkness and the bleak fields of snow. It was a hard, cruel country, and after a time the temperament of the people living in it seemed to take on the qualities of the barren land. So many hatreds and conflicts in this small village! She had never dreamed life in this lumber village would be anything like it was.

It was dark outside by the time Charles emerged from the bathroom. He went about dressing, and she noted that his limp was now less pronounced.

"Did the hot tub help?" she asked.

"Yes," he said as he tied his tie before the mirror. "I feel a lot better."

"Remember to use the cane," she said. "Even when you're around the house."

He turned to her with a weary smile as he put on his jacket. "I will. Maybe David will accept that I'm also crippled now. He has refused to believe it up to this point. A cane may convince him."

She said, "I had a long talk with David this afternoon."

"You did?" her husband was surprised.

"Yes."

He sat on the arm of one of the bedroom's two easy chairs and asked, "How did you manage that?"

"I caught him at a moment when he was bored with the wireless."

"I didn't know he had such moments."

"He does," she assured him. "I think I managed to make him understand my feelings. That I want to be his friend."

"No doubt he insulted you!" Charles said bitterly.

"Not badly," she said with a feeble smile.

"I can't promise you that it's worth it," Charles said. "I'm almost ready to give up on him. I've considered talking to him and offering to set him up in an apartment somewhere in a city of his choice. Maybe on his own he'd be happier."

She felt a sudden twinge of fear for the handsome boy in the wheelchair. She said, "No. I don't like that idea. I think it would be cruel to send him off alone."

"He isn't happy here."

"Give it a little more time," she said.

He shrugged. "If you like. We'd better go

down. The others will be waiting for us."

She got him his cane and they went down the stairs together. They found Mabel and Ned having drinks in the living room. At Ned's request they joined them. Mabel at once commented on Charles using a cane and entered into a discussion with him about his leg.

She found herself in Ned's company as they sipped their before-dinner drinks. Her husband's younger brother said, "There is a good program on the French television tonight. A ballet done by a top Parisian company. We ought to watch it."

"I'd like to," she said.

Ned gave her a rather strange look and said, "I hear you had an adventurous afternoon."

"Almost too adventurous," she said.

Ned's eyes were fixed on hers. "You ought to reconsider and make that trip to Montreal with Mabel tomorrow. It would give you a change."

"No," she said. "It's too soon yet." She thought she knew why the serious Ned was so anxious to have someone with his young blonde wife. He probably suspected that she was having an affair with somebody on her overnight trips. Having a chaperone along might hinder this.

"I can't see why," he argued.

"Perhaps another time," she said, putting him off with a smile. She had no desire to become embroiled in the marital problems of the two.

At dinner the atmosphere was rather tense. Mabel talked too much and Ned too little. And Charles seemed to be in a grim, preoccupied state, which didn't help matters any. She felt a sense of relief when they finally rose from the table. At Ned's suggestion they all settled down in a darkened living room to watch the televised ballet program from Montreal.

It was the classic *Swan Lake*, and while Lucy was familiar with it she found it well done and thoroughly absorbing. In fact she became so lost in the music and dance that she forgot her surroundings. It was only during a station break when Mabel reached over and touched her shoulder that she came back to reality.

The blonde leaned to her in the darkness and said, "You've lost your husband."

She stared at her blankly. "What?"

"Come with me," Mabel said with a wise look on her pretty face.

The ballet was resuming but she was now disturbed, so she got up and went with her sister-in-law, leaving Ned sitting alone before the color television in the darkened living room.

Mabel quickly led her up the right stairway and then along the corridor to the door to the attic and the room that Sheila had used as a studio. Mabel paused before the open door.

With a triumphant smile on her lovely face she told Lucy, with a hint of sarcasm, "He's up there with her again!"

Chapter Six

It was impossible to miss the implication of the blonde girl's taunting words. Lucy stood there in the near darkness gazing up at the stairway that led to the studio above. And she recalled that when they had talked at the hospital, Mabel had mentioned the weird visits Charles paid to the upper room. She had mentioned how strange his preoccupation with the studio had been. And so he was up there now.

In a low voice, she said, "I didn't hear him leave the room."

"I saw him go," Mabel said. "He was careful not to draw our attention."

"Does this happen often?"

"Often enough," the other girl said. "I thought you ought to know."

"Thank you," she said bleakly.

Mabel eyed her with morbid interest. "Are you going up there to him?"

She shook her head. "Why should I? He obviously wants to be alone."

"I don't think it's healthy."

"Whatever we may think I consider it his business," she said shortly. "Now I say we should go back downstairs."

"If you want to," Mabel replied grudgingly. It was clear that she had hoped for some sort of confrontation between them.

Lucy led the way back down to the living room and took her chair to watch the rest of the television show. Ned gave her and Mabel a glance as they rejoined him, but said nothing. For a time they sat watching the remainder of the ballet. Lucy put on a show of casualness, but she had a hard time keeping her mind on the ballet.

She'd not wanted to give Mabel the satisfaction of knowing she was upset, but the incident had troubled her a good deal. She could not understand why Charles should be obsessed with that upper room at this point. Shortly after Sheila's death it would have been understandable. But too much time had passed. His behaving like this now could only suggest a guilty conscience.

Trying not to think about it, she forced herself to give more attention to the ballet. At last it ended, and Ned got up and turned on the lights and switched off the television set. The Prentiss family watched the television only when a special program was offered. They were not fans in the regular sense of the word.

He said, "I enjoyed that."

"It was fine," she agreed.

Mabel got to her feet with a bored look. "I'm sleepy now," she announced. "I must get straight to bed, since I'll be making that flight early in the morning."

Ned gave her a sober look. "Do you really have to make this trip to Montreal?"

"Indeed I do!" she snapped. "Aside from making all those trips to Portland when Charles was in the hospital, I've scarcely had a day away from here! I need a change!"

"Very well," he said placatingly. And he turned to Lucy, "It seems we lost Charles. I have an idea he's not a ballet lover."

"Apparently not," she said in a wry voice. "I think it is time for me to go to bed as well."

"It is getting late," Ned agreed as he glanced at his wristwatch.

They all made their way upstairs and said their good-nights. When Lucy reached their bedroom she hoped that Charles would be there, but he wasn't. She slowly began preparing for bed.

She was in her nightgown and sitting up

in bed when her husband came into the room. He was using his cane and when he saw her he at once looked apologetic and a little guilty.

He said, "I'm sorry I missed the program."

Her eyes met his. "It was your own choice."

"I know," he sighed. "You must forgive me."

He began to move around preparing for bed. She decided not to question him further until he came to her bedside to kiss her goodnight. When he did, she asked him, "Why did you do it?"

The uneasy expression crossed his face again. He said, "I lost interest in the program."

"I can understand that," she said. "But why did you decide to go up there?"

He avoided looking at her, staring down at the carpet between the twin beds. He said, "I don't know. Call it an impulse. All Sheila's last work is still up there. I thought I'd like to look around the place."

"And so you went up there by yourself and sat for several hours," she said. "Do you call that a normal thing to do?"

He frowned at her. "What's abnormal about it?"

"Your secrecy. And your staying up there so long."

He raised a hand in protest. "You'll have to be patient with me. Believe me, this was nothing."

"You say that."

"It's true."

"Linking yourself to a dead wife is morbid," she said with a worried look.

"I can't explain more," he said with enough obstinacy to make her convinced he meant it.

So when he got into his own bed and turned out the lights, this difference was still between them. She lay very still in bed, feeling actual pain about it all. The wind had come up, as it so frequently did at night, and was whistling bleakly about the great lodge. Its planks groaned and creaked in the cold winter night. At last she fell into a troubled sleep.

She was wakened by Charles calling out as if in pain. It frightened her, and she quickly sat up in bed and stared across at him in the darkness with a troubled expression on her pretty face. Through the shadows she saw him twist unhappily under the bedclothes, and then he began talking in his sleep. It was a tortured rambling, and she could make out only an occasional word of what he was saying.

Straining, she was able to clearly hear "stairs," and later, "house," along with "trees" and his late wife's name again, "Sheila." Then the words became so garbled and infrequent that she could make nothing of them. As he eased back into a sound sleep, she found herself upset and awake. She sat in bed watching him for a while longer, but there was just the gentle sound of his breathing.

Now she rose from the bed and put on her dressing gown. She had no idea what she intended to do, but she was too restless to remain there attempting sleep. She moved slowly across the room and gazed out the window at the winter night. It was snowing a little and blowing. She almost began to sympathize with Mabel and her complaints about the bleakness of the place.

She went to the door, quietly opened it, and stepped into the corridor. It came to her that her husband might not have locked up that studio room, and so she might have a chance to go up and see what was up there. With this in mind she went down the corridor toward the door to the stairs and the studio above.

When she reached the door she tried the

knob and found that it was locked. He'd been careful to do that before returning to her, she thought bitterly. What ghostly secret did that room hold that he clung to it so? Why couldn't he tell her what it meant to him? It was a troublesome business.

She was thinking these things when suddenly she felt a chill burst of air whip around hers. It was an eerie experience, as if she were being enveloped by some cold, ghostly cloak. It made her tremble, and she wondered if it had anything to do with her attempted assault on this citadel of the dead Sheila.

Drawing away from the door in fear, she let her eyes wander to the end of the corridor by the balcony. It was then she saw it again. The same ghostly form she'd seen on that first night she'd come to the old lodge, now framed against the soft glow of the tiny night light on the balcony. The phantom figure of Sheila!

And then, as it had before, it vanished! She hesitated a moment, and then summoning all her courage slowly advanced down the corridor to the balcony. She took what seemed an endless time to make the short journey. And when she finally reached the spot where she'd seen the phantom figure, there was no sign of anyone.

She stood on the balcony gazing down into the shadow of the living room. A few embers still glowed in the fireplace from the fire they'd had earlier in the evening. She was still trembling and fearful. A footstep sounded behind her, and she whirled around with a tiny cry! It was the housekeeper, Mrs. Warren, in a heavy dark robe.

The housekeeper stared at her. "I thought I heard someone out here."

"I wasn't able to sleep," she said awkwardly.

Mrs. Warren nodded. "The wind is wicked tonight. It woke me up, otherwise I wouldn't have heard you."

"Sorry to be a nuisance," she apologized.

"Not at all," the older woman said. "I can understand. You're not used to this place and the way it complains in the wind."

"No. I'm not."

The gray-haired woman said, "Would you like a hot drink or anything?"

She shook her head. "No. I'll go back to bed in a minute. I may be able to sleep now."

"I hope so," Mrs. Warren said sympathetically.

Lucy said goodnight to her and walked

down to the bedroom she shared with Charles. It had been an eerie experience and she'd made a spectacle of herself, but fortunately Mrs. Warren had seemed to understand. She hadn't dared mention the phantom figure to the housekeeper. It wouldn't have done any good. Nor could she mention it to Charles. He would simply become angry and insist she was imagining things again. But she knew what she had seen!

Charles was still sleeping peacefully when she returned to her bed. She was in no mood for sleep. But eventually sheer weariness took over and her eyes closed. She enjoyed an uneasy rest until morning. When she woke Charles had already gone. She wearily got up and dressed for breakfast.

She had the table to herself. And when Mrs. Warren came into the dining room she asked, "Did the other Mrs. Prentiss get away as she planned?"

"Yes," the prim woman said. "She left about a half-hour ago. Her husband drove her to the airfield."

"That should get her to Montreal early."

"By midmorning," Mrs. Warren said.

"At least she has good weather for the flight, even though there were some snow flurries last night."

The prim housekeeper nodded. "Yes. It's fine this morning. Did you manage to get back to sleep?"

She forced a smile. "I did. I must have seemed a sorry sight to you wandering about like that."

"No, madam," Mrs. Warren said. "It was a bad wind."

"It was," she agreed. "Has my husband left for the mill?"

"Yes."

"I must go and visit it soon," she said. "I've never been inside it yet."

"It's quite a sight," Mrs. Warren admitted. "Biggest buildings in the village and full of noisy equipment. I declare it's a wonder the men working there don't get deaf."

"I can imagine," she said.

"In these villages the church is sometimes the largest building you'll see, but not in Seven Timbers. We have a joke among ourselves and say we worship at the mill instead of the church."

She smiled. "Well, it seems to be the center of the community. Where is the church?"

"In the village on the back street. It's small and you'd hardly notice it. We only have services here every second Sunday. The priest comes up on the morning train and leaves on the night one."

"I see," she said.

Mrs. Warren was in one of her talkative moods. She said, "But a few of the families here don't go to the church. The Prentiss family, along with the Rhode family and some others, don't have any church. They have to visit some other place to attend a service."

"That is rather difficult," she said.

"Yes. When they have weddings they must bring a minister in. And the same with funerals. And they have a private burial ground not far from the lodge. It's on the hill directly behind it. All the Prentiss family is buried there, and the Rhodes, as well as a lot of the servants. Like as not I'll be buried there one day."

Lucy found herself asking tautly, "Is Sheila buried there?"

Mrs. Warren looked at her oddly. "Yes, madam," she said in a solemn voice. "And it's my opinion she lies in an uneasy grave. At least that's what you'd think from the stories about her phantom walking here in the night."

"I know," she said.

"I'll get the maid started serving you," Mrs. Warren said, and hurried off toward the kitchen.

She remained seated at the table. In the distance she heard the mournful wail of a train whistle. And then the sound of the freight rumbling by as it passed through the village below. She could not argue that Sheila was uneasy in her grave, since she was sure she had seen the phantom again the previous night.

When she finished breakfast she went upstairs again and decided to pay David a visit. The youth was busy at his wireless set when she entered the tiny room. But he did her the courtesy of quickly finishing his conversation and turning the set off. Then he gave her a questioning look. "Why did you come here?" he asked.

"To visit with you."

"Do you find that so pleasant?"

"Why not?" she said. "I'm lonely."

He frowned at her. "Why should you be? You can go where you like and do as you please!"

She shook her head. "You know that's not true."

"You aren't chained to a wheelchair!"

"There are other things that bind us," she said. "No one has complete freedom. And I certainly don't. I'm trying to adjust to this place and I find it difficult."

"My mother loved Seven Timbers," he

said defiantly. "You've seen all her paintings of the place."

"The walls are filled with them," she agreed. "And in a way she continues to live in those paintings."

He stared at her in surprise. "You think that?"

"Yes. Art is a form of immortality. At least one of the minor forms of which we weak creatures are capable. Your mother will always live in this house as long as her paintings hang here."

David's boyish face was all surprise. "And you don't resent that?"

"Why should I?"

"I'd expect you'd go around tearing them down. I thought you would have had them removed long ago!"

She smiled. "Never. I wouldn't dream of doing anything like that. Why should I?"

The boy looked baffled. "I don't know. I guess I expected you would hate my mother."

"You think of people hating far too easily," she said. "I'd try to get over that."

The boy stared at her. He said, "You aren't making it easy for me to hate you."

"I'm glad of that," she said. "I want us to be friends. I won't keep you from your wireless pals any longer." And with a parting smile she left him.

She felt that she was gradually winning him over to accept her. It wasn't done yet, and it might take a good deal of time, but she was on the way. And it was such a worthwhile project. The most important thing she could do at Seven Timbers, it seemed. She also wanted to make her husband's lot easier, but that apparently was going to be more difficult. Charles was more neurotically twisted than his son.

It was a fine day, and being trapped in the old mansion made her feel edgy. So she donned her ski outfit and the heavy woolen hat and started out again. She strolled around the grounds of the lodge and discovered there was a large, kidney-shaped swimming pool at its rear. She inspected it and saw that it was frozen over. It struck her that David could use this to good advantage in the summer. The exercise he'd get in the pool should be extremely helpful in restoring his leg muscles.

As she was standing by the pool she looked up and saw, on the hill above, the dark, tapered peak of a tall monument. She remembered Mrs. Warren telling her about the family graveyard and decided it must be up there. So she made her way around the pool and up the hill to the spot where she'd seen the stone.

Reaching the summit of the hill she saw the graveyard stretch out before her. It was on a section of high, flat land of the sort favored for burials. And it was dotted with gravestones large and small. The burial ground had been divided into lots, and she walked through it until she came to the Prentiss lot.

At this high point the wind was strong and she coiled her coat around her and folded her arms to hold it protectively. Then she began studying the various headstones. The most ancient of the gray stones showed the toll of the winds and rain over the years. She was barely able to decipher it, but she did discover that the first male Prentiss had been buried there in 1869.

There were a number of other stones of various years and then the newer ones. It took her only a moment to locate the black marble marker over Sheila's grave. It was modest but good-looking and simply noted the dates of her birth and death, and beneath them were the words, "Beloved wife and mother." That was it. The summing up of the attractive woman's thirty-seven years!

As Lucy stood there shivering slightly and studying the snow-capped mound that marked the grave, she had the weird feeling that Sheila was not there beneath the frozen earth but still back in the great, rambling lodge in which she'd lived so long. She could not explain why she felt this way, but it was as if she were standing by an empty grave!

She lifted her eyes from the tombstone and saw that she was now on a level with the upper door of the lodge. And to her surprise she saw a figure at one of the windows, apparently watching her. This served to increase her uneasy feelings. At such a distance she could not tell who it might be, but she was sure she was being observed. A curtain flicked and the figure vanished, leaving her with a whole new set of questions.

After a moment longer by Sheila's grave she walked back down to the pool area again. And then she decided to pay a visit to the mill. She hoped that Charles might be there and that he would show her through it. She walked the fairly long distance to the first of the buildings and was aware of the curious stares given her by the men unloading lumber trucks outside.

Entering the office of the mill, which was in the largest of the connected buildings, she found herself at a high, old-style wooden counter. A number of men and women were working at desks behind it, and one of them came to greet her.

The young woman asked, "Yes?"

"I'm Mrs. Prentiss," she said. "I'd like to see my husband."

The girl looked embarrassed. "Mrs. Charles Prentiss?"

She smiled. "Yes. I'm the new Mrs. Prentiss."

The girl relaxed and smiled in return. "How do you do, Mrs. Prentiss. I'm new here, so I wasn't sure. I'm afraid your husband has gone to the junction. They are having problems up there."

"Oh!" she said, disappointed.

"Mr. Ned Prentiss is in his office," the girl suggested helpfully.

"Is he?"

"Yes. Would you like to see him?"

"I suppose so," she said. "Tell him who it is."

"One moment," the girl said. And she vanished through a doorway at the rear of the large office. Lucy waited there, conscious that many of the desk workers were furtively taking glances at her. She supposed her marriage to Charles had provided gossip for the remote village for quite a spell.

Then Ned suddenly appeared through the doorway, followed by the girl. He came over to her with a smile on his normally serious face and said, "You decided to come and see us, after all."

"Yes," she said. "But I've apparently chosen a bad time."

"Not at all," Ned said. "Charles isn't here. We're having loading troubles at the junction and he's gone up to troubleshoot."

"I see."

"But I'll show you through the place briefly," her husband's younger brother said. "Then Charles can give you a royal tour later on."

"There's no need!" she protested.

"I'd like to do it," he said.

He went up to the end of the counter and lifted a section of it to let her through. Then he guided her past the desks in the big office and out through to the back. There was a corridor with various private offices leading from it and another door at the end that had a white sign with black lettering: MILL. It was through this door he took her.

She suddenly found herself in a bedlam of sound and activity. The mill was probably three stories high and was filled with equipment. The pungent smell of wood freshly cut filled the air like a fine spice. And the screeching of great logs as they were cut into planks rose high above all the other sounds. She saw the men in their blue uniforms and caps busy at the various machines. And at a second level she saw fresh lumber stacked, waiting to dry out and be shipped.

Ned kept a hand on her arm and guided her through the modern inferno of equipment and men. He made no attempt to shout any explanations. She wouldn't have heard him in any case. But he did give her a complete tour of the massive operation before he escorted her back to the comparative silence of the office section once again.

In the corridor he said, "Come into my office for a few minutes until you're back to normal."

"That noise!" she laughed.

"I know," he agreed. "It takes getting used to." He guided her into a large, pleasant office with a wall lined with bound order files. There was a clutter of magazines and catalogues on his desk along with some opened mail. He had her sit across from him and opened a drawer in the desk and brought out a bottle and glasses. "I'd say you needed a drink."

"Not really," she said.

"Mind if I have one?" he asked.

"Of course not," she said. And it struck her that he might have the habit of often treating himself in this fashion. She'd not realized it before but Ned had the look of a hard drinker.

"Important occasion," he said, splashing the liquor generously in the big glass. "Have to mark it!" And he got up and went over to the washbasin in the corner of the room and filled the glass partway with water. Then he came back to his chair behind the desk and took a good gulp from the glass.

"It's a large mill," she said.

He nodded. "Built up over the years. The last building was added about five years ago. I don't think there will be any others."

"Oh?"

Ned took another drink. "No one in the family to carry on after Charles and I give up. David might have considered it at one time, but that's over now. This was always a family business. We'll probably sell out to some larger firm, and the Prentiss Mill will continue to exist merely as a name and a unit of a larger operation."

"It seems rather sad," she said. "I've

166

come here directly from your family burial ground."

He smiled at her. "Seen some of the names of the old boys!"

"Yes. I think there was a Prentiss buried there in 1869."

"Right," he said, taking another drink. "That was our great-grandfather. He was the one who found this village and made up his mind it would make a good spot for a mill."

"He made no mistake."

"True," Ned Prentiss said with a forlorn look. "But Mabel doesn't think so. She hates this place."

"That's too bad."

"It is for me," he said. "She thinks I should retire and move somewhere else and play the role of country gentleman." He shook his head. "Retire at thirty-six! My father made the biggest improvement in the operations of the mill after he was my age."

"I'm sure he did."

Ned finished the liquor with another gulp and stared at the glass thoughtfully. "Helps you through the day."

She smiled. "I doubt that you need help."

"I do today," he said. "Mabel is back in

Montreal again. There are times when I'm sorry we have our own planes. I think she might not want to make so many trips if she had to travel in the last car of the freight trains running through here."

"That might cure her," she said.

"I doubt it," he sighed. "She'd just up and leave me." He gave her a direct look. "Charles is the lucky one. He found Sheila, and when he lost her he found you."

"I'm beginning to wonder if he is all that lucky," she said. "I'm not sure that I'm fitting in as well as I might."

"What can you expect? You've only been here a few days."

"Rather hectic days. And Charles doesn't seem in a good frame of mind."

Ned's eyebrows rose. "How do you mean? He's using his cane today. I thought he never would."

"I'm glad of that," she said. "But that's not what I meant."

"No?"

"No. You must have noticed that he left us last night when we were watching the ballet."

Her brother-in-law nodded. "Yes. But then you and Mabel also deserted me for a little. I guess I'm the only ballet fan."

"It wasn't a question of not wanting to

watch the ballet," she said. "Mabel took me upstairs to let me know where Charles was."

Ned frowned. "And where was he?"

"He'd unlocked the door to the studio stairway and he was up there."

Her husband's brother showed an uneasiness. He said, "Did you go up to him?"

"No. I felt that I shouldn't."

"And?"

"We came back down again."

Ned looked angry. "I think Mabel might have let that pass. I don't see what was gained by her letting you know he was up there."

"It's nothing new, is it?" she asked carefully. "I mean he often goes up there, doesn't he?"

The man behind the desk hesitated. "Yes, he does."

"Why?"

"You should ask him."

"I did."

"And?"

"He refused to tell me," she said. "He seemed quite tormented about it."

Ned eyed her grimly and then got up from behind the desk. Putting his hands in his trousers pockets, he began to pace slowly up and down before her. He shook his head and stared at the floor.

At last he said, "Charles is my brother. But I'll be frank with you. I don't understand him. And since Sheila's death he has been doubly hard to get along with."

"He seems to be hiding something about her or her death," she worried.

"I don't know what it is," Ned said. "It began with David's accident, of course."

"That must have been a bad blow."

"You have no idea," Ned said. "When the boy came back I began to hope it would be all right again, but it wasn't."

"I suppose that was when they learned he couldn't walk."

"He did get around on crutches for awhile. But Sheila didn't handle that too well. Every time she saw David on crutches she started to cry. After some of that the boy began to stay in his wheelchair. Funny, that didn't seem to bother her nearly so much."

"But it would have been better for him to keep on using the crutches," she said. "Just how bad was his injury?"

"The spinal cord wasn't completely severed, but it was damaged a good deal," Ned Prentiss said. "The doctors at the clinic felt in time and with exercise he might gain a fair degree of use of his legs.

That's why Charles put in the swimming pool."

"Has it been used?" she asked.

Standing looking out the window of his office, Ned said, "Only at the start. Then David took to his wheelchair and that damned wireless set. It has been the ruination of him!"

"It must have helped him in a way."

"Made him a recluse. He hardly ever leaves that room now."

"I know," she said.

"He used to come down to dinner on his crutches. But Sheila would start her silent crying, and after a little he had his meals sent up to him. He still does."

"I know."

"Sheila meant to be a good wife and mother, but after David's accident I can't say that she was."

"I'm beginning to realize that," Lucy said. "Of course she meant to be."

"Good intentions!" Ned said with disgust and began pacing again. "And then there were the continual quarrels between Charles and her."

"They were really bad?"

"Kept the house in a turmoil," he said. "Sheila insisted that it was carelessness on Charles' part that caused the accident."

171

"Even if she were right she didn't accomplish anything by harping on it afterwards. I'm sure Charles didn't want the accident to happen."

Ned looked at her evenly. "I know my brother well enough to say he would rather have died himself."

"I'm sure of that."

"But Sheila didn't forgive him. She kept on nagging. And I'd say she turned David against him. That's when I first realized that Charles was changing. That his mental state was bad."

"Couldn't you talk to her? Point out what was happening? That she was destroying her husband!"

Ned halted before her. He nodded. "I tried that. And she told me it wasn't any of my business."

"She had no pity for him?"

"Not an ounce. And all the while I saw Charles failing. He lost weight and his nerves were bad."

"And then?" Lucy said.

Ned said, "Just when I was wondering how long Charles could stand up to it, Sheila had her accident."

"So she was silenced in the only way possible."

"Silenced by fate!" Ned agreed. "Both

Charles and I were away from the house. I was in the next village. We'd had a fire in one of the camps and I went up to see how bad the damage was. Charles was working in the office and waiting for me."

"Who found her?"

"I came back here and reported to Charles," his brother said. "Then we both started for the lodge. He went in first and found her, but I was there almost the same moment."

"She was already dead?"

"Yes. But Charles sent for the doctor."

"Who was in the house when it happened?"

"David and Mabel, of the family," Ned said. "He was too busy at his wireless to hear anything. Mabel was in bed with a sick headache and under sedation. So it happened without her knowing."

"What about Mrs. Warren?"

"Out visiting someone. And the other servants live in a part of the house too far away to hear anything. So we don't know what happened that night. I think maybe it was a lucky thing. It may have saved Charles."

She said, "He's still in a bad state."

"I know that," Ned said. And after a moment's hesitation he added, "That accident he had when he hurt his leg. Mabel was there with him. She says it wasn't any accident. That he let himself fall off the platform. It was a suicide attempt!"

Chapter Seven

Lucy had long been worried about her husband's mental health, and this rather shocking statement only served to underline her worst fears. The circumstances of his accident, like those surrounding the death of Sheila, remained blurred in mystery. She gave Charles' younger brother a frightened look.

"Do you honestly think that? That Charles meant to take his life?" she asked.

Ned spread his hands in a gesture of resignation. "I don't know. I have moments when I think yes, and then I decide no. It is hard to be certain."

"That's the way I've felt," she said.

He gave her a meaningful look. "I can tell you one thing. I have a valuable collection of old guns, as you know."

"Yes."

"I keep them in a locked room in the cellar. And I've been especially careful of them since noticing this change in Charles. I intend to make sure he never gets his hands on any of them. There have been too many accidental deaths from old weapons of that sort. It would be an ideal way of suicide for him."

She nodded worriedly. "You're right. I'd never thought of that."

Ned sighed and walked back to his desk and stood behind it. "I'm very fond of Charles. We get along fairly well. And though he is only a couple of years older than I am, he has always been a sort of father image to me."

"I understand," she said.

"We'll have to hope that he gets over this depression and comes back to his normal self again," Ned said.

"Let us hope so," she agreed. "I think a great deal depends on David. If he should come back to better health, Charles wouldn't feel so guilty."

"I agree."

She said, "I've tried to be friendly with the boy and encourage him to be more active. I think I may be getting somewhere. He will talk with me now."

Ned's pleasant face showed a frown. "I hope you won't have the same experience as Mabel."

She stared at him. "What experience did she have?"

"She made friendly overtures to him, and for awhile she spent quite a lot of time up in his wireless room. He had a sort of boyish crush on her."

"Mabel is very attractive. And young," she agreed.

"But the magic of the relationship soon vanished," the young man standing at the desk said. "Ended disastrously."

"Really?"

"Yes. He turned against her at the time of his mother's death."

"I can understand that," Lucy said. "He would automatically resent anyone who he thought might be trying to take his mother's place."

"That may have been it. Anyway, Mabel claimed he was rude to her. Turned his back on her and refused to talk."

"Did she keep on trying?"

"Yes. It was no good. So now she doesn't go up there at all. They rarely see each other."

"I know," she said. "I had no idea they had been fairly close at one time. David didn't say anything about it."

"He's almost psychotic," Ned Prentiss worriedly commented on his nephew.

177

"I worry about him," she said. "Not only for his own sake but for his father's."

"I understand," Ned said. "And I agree a happier David would surely mean a happier Charles."

"I'll keep on talking with David as long as he'll allow it," she said. "Perhaps he won't have the same resentment toward me he showed to Mabel. I wasn't in the house when his mother was alive."

"That is a plus," her husband's brother agreed.

She got up from her chair. "I've stayed too long."

"Not at all," he said. "We have plenty to talk about."

"That is true. And for the most part we get so little time."

He smiled wearily as he escorted her out. "I spend most of my hours away from the business catering to Mabel and trying to make her happy here. It appears I'm not doing too well."

She said, "I'd let her have her trips to Montreal if they mean so much to her. Then she is more content with this place on her return."

"I've gone along with it because of thinking exactly that," Ned said.

"I'd say you were wise."

"Time will tell," he said, not sounding all that sure about it.

She went out through the main office again and on to the mill yard, where trucks were continually arriving, unloading, and leaving. The activity at the mill had impressed her, and the long talk she'd enjoyed with Ned had filled her in on a number of things she hadn't been sure about before.

The suggestion that Charles might be suicidal did not surprise her, though it caused her new concern. She was amazed to know that Mabel and young David had once been friendly. There was no hint of it now.

She walked back up the snow-covered road to the big lodge, which dominated the village. Viewed in the sunlight it did not seem a sinister place at all. And yet she was finding it so. She felt that it seethed with tensions and was filled with unsolved mysteries — not the least of them the business of Sheila's ghost!

Once again last night she'd seen the furtive shadow, and when she'd visited the graveside of her dead predecessor she'd had that strange, haunting sensation that Sheila was not buried there. It made her wonder.

Reaching the lodge she had luncheon alone. And when she finished she decided to go up to David's room and see how the youth was making out. She went up the stairs and took the corridor down to the wireless room. Once again he was seated in somber thought, with the wireless turned off.

She went in and said, "You're taking a rest again."

"Nothing interesting on the wire," he said.

Her eyebrows lifted. "I thought you always found the wireless absorbing."

David gave her a rather annoyed look. "I guess you can get tired of anything."

"That is true," she agreed.

"Where were you this morning?"

"I visited the mill. My first time."

The youth's face brightened. "It's quite a set-up, isn't it?"

"Fascinating. I can understand why Charles and Ned are so dedicated to it."

"When my great-grandfather ran it the mill was small," he said. "My grandfather and my father and uncle built it up the way it is."

"It will be yours one day," she reminded him.

David took on a sullen look again. "Never."

"Why not?"

"There's no room for a cripple in running an active business like that," he protested.

"Who can tell? You may not always be crippled."

He gave her a grim smile. "I wouldn't count on that."

"Your uncle and Mabel have no children, and it's not likely they will have," she said. "So there is only you. If you don't carry on, the business will surely pass from family hands."

"Mabel!" he said in a disgusted tone.

"I understand you and she were great friends at one time," she said, making up her mind to challenge him on the subject. "What happened between you?"

He eyed her warily. "Who told you that?"

"Ned."

"Oh?" He seemed less resentful.

"What made you become angry with Mabel?"

Again he showed uneasiness. "What gives you the idea I'm angry with her?"

"She says you are."

"I just don't want her for a friend!"

"You did once."

"She came up here and pretended to be friendly and told me a lot of lies," the boy said resentfully.

"I can't imagine why. Are you sure you aren't being unfair to her?"

"She thought she'd take my mother's place," David said. "And she did. But not with me. But she took over the house until you came."

"And now she's handed the running of it over to me," she said.

David's young face took on a warning look. "Don't let that fool you! She probably hates you!"

"I don't think so," she said with a smile. "At any rate I'm not worried."

"Better not be friendly with her," the youth went on. "She'll only try to trick you like she did me."

She frowned. "Why do you say that?"

"She was never my friend," David said almost fiercely. "She only pretended. And I don't want to ever have anything to do with her again."

"That's all right with me," she assured him. "I'm not trying to push Mabel's cause with you. I'm content that you are willing to be my friend."

"I didn't want to at first," he told her.

"I know."

"But now I can see you are more honest than most of the others in this house, and that includes my father."

She stared at the boy's angry face. "You don't care much for him, do you?"

"No. And maybe you won't by the time you leave here."

She said, "You expect me to leave here?"

"Yes."

"Why?"

"My mother will force you to go," was his simply said yet shocking reply.

She hesitated before making any comment on this. Then for want of something better, she said, "Your mother happens to be dead."

An almost crafty look crossed the face that was so much a younger version of her husband's, and the boy said, "Maybe so, but she still has power in this house."

"I see," she said.

"You don't believe me," David said, studying her.

"I didn't say that."

"I can tell."

"Let's say I'm willing to be convinced," she told him.

"You will be," David said. "I don't think she'll harm you, but you'll not want to stay here."

She said, "You're a strange boy, David. You have a lot of very weird ideas. I think you spend too much time in here alone."

"I do what I like," he said, the sullenness returning again.

"I gather that," she said. "But sometimes doing what we like isn't always best for us." And once again she made a point of leaving while she still had the last word.

As evidence that she had bothered him she heard the ham radio turned on once more as she walked down the hall away from the tiny room. Ned had voiced the opinion earlier in the day that he worried about David becoming psychotic. Judging by her conversation with him just now, it seemed all too likely that his young mind was already tinged with madness.

She spent some time in her bedroom that afternoon altering a dress that was a favorite of hers. It was a knit with gold thread and needed to be hemmed. She'd barely finished this and put it away when Charles arrived. He came into the room with his cane in hand and crossed over to give her a kiss.

She smiled as she stood with her arm around him. "At least you are using the cane."

"Not much choice," he said with a weary smile on his handsome face. "The leg bothers me when I don't use it."

"I visited the mill today," she said.

"Ned told me," her husband said as he went over to one of the easy chairs and sat down. "I'm sorry I wasn't there."

"He gave me quite a good tour of the place."

"He'd enjoy that," Charles said. "It would be nice for him if Mabel took more interest in the mill."

She was sitting across from him on the edge of one of the beds. She said, "She was there with you the day you had your accident, wasn't she?"

Charles' face clouded. "That was an exception. She rarely goes down there."

"I see," she said. "Ned and I had a long talk. He's very nice, but I can see he's worried about Mabel being so dissatisfied with living here."

"That's not apt to change," Charles said. "It might be better if they would decide to break up and he'd give her a divorce."

"Is it that bad?"

"It's bad enough," her husband said.

"But she was brought up here."

"Her family were poor, maybe that's why she resents the place so. It's hard to tell."

"I also heard that she and David had been good friends and then he'd suddenly turned away from her."

Charles gave her a tragic look. "Are you

surprised? He has turned his back on everyone."

"I think he needs psychiatric help," she suggested.

"I discussed that with him," Charles said. "I got nowhere."

"Maybe I could try."

"Try if you like," her husband said, "but don't expect to have him agree."

"I'm afraid he's going to become a mental case unless he has the proper help," she argued.

Charles shrugged. "I hope not."

"You'll have to do better than that," she said. "Why not bring a psychiatrist down here?"

"I'm not sure David would talk to him."

"It would be worth a try," she said.

"I'll think about it," her husband promised. "I have to work at the office tonight. And tomorrow I have to go to New York. I'll go as soon as Ben Huggard flies Mabel back in the morning. When I'm in New York I'll try and discuss David with a reputable psychiatrist."

"That would be very wise," she said.

"Then we can decide whether to bring one here or not," her husband said.

"I'll try and get him ready for the idea in the meantime," she said.

Charles gave her a warning glance. "Don't make it too obvious. He is quick to catch on. If he thinks you're preparing some sort of trap for him he'll really turn on you, just as he did on Mabel."

"I realize that," she said. And she again noted the tension in her husband's manner and the lines of worry in his face. She felt sure that if the problem of David could be solved, everyone would be happier.

Yet she could not close her eyes to the grim truths about Charles himself. Charles, who chose to lock himself in the studio of his dead wife for hours. Charles, who very likely had made at least one attempt at suicide! Was he in a fit state to decide about treatment?

She said, "Will you be gone overnight when you make the New York trip?"

"Yes," he said. "You won't mind, will you? Mabel will be back. And there's Ned and David in the house to keep you company."

"I'll manage," she said.

"I'd have you come along," he told her, "but it is strictly a business trip. I have appointments even in the late afternoon and evening. And if I try to look into this psychiatrist matter, I won't have a free minute."

"I understand," she said.

Charles sighed. "I'll try and get back as early as possible the following day."

That night there were only herself, Charles, and Ned at the dinner table. Charles and Ned talked business a good deal of the time, and when the meal ended they both returned to the office to prepare some material that Charles proposed to take to New York with him. This left her alone.

She went to the window of the living room overlooking the front lawns and saw that it was snowing again. It struck her that it had been snowing most of the time since she'd arrived at Seven Timbers. And she thought of Mabel among the bright lights of distant Montreal and wondered what she was doing.

After a little she grew tired of being alone and decided that she'd go up and pay David a short visit. She knew there was a risk in seeing him too often, but she also felt that he was very lonely and so might not resent her intruding on him again. For a seventeen-year-old he had a strong sense of dignity.

As she made her way down the corridor to his room she all at once realized that the wireless was not on. This didn't surprise her, since there had been a number of times lately when he'd turned it off. She hoped this was an encouraging sign. But as she reached the doorway of the room she was startled to discover that he wasn't there! His wheelchair was there, but there was no sign of David!

This shocked her so that she stood there for a full moment staring at the empty chair. Then she began to experience a mild panic as she worried what might have happened to the troubled youth. She debated whether she should try to find Mrs. Warren and search for him or phone the mill and let Charles know what had happened.

She tried to tell herself she was making too much of it, but she still worried. Stepping inside the tiny room she searched for something that might give a clue to where he'd gone, but there was nothing. And how could he manage to get about without his wheelchair? She stared at the empty wheelchair in dismay.

After she recovered from the initial shock of her discovery, she went out into the corridor and checked all the nearby rooms. There was no sign of the missing David. Now she went out into the balcony and gazed down into the living room. No hint of him there. She decided to try another area, and she hurried down the other corridor to the door that led to the studio stairway. And as she had surmised, the door was unlocked and open.

The shadowed stairway leading to the studio tempted her. She was now almost certain that David was up there, and she was anxious to see the place for herself. She fixed her eyes on the slit of light under the doorway at the head of the stairway and felt herself trembling. Something told her that behind that door lay much of the mystery upsetting the old house.

She mounted the stairs slowly, her heart throbbing with excitement as she listened for some sound from above. Any sound! Then, finally, she was at the top stair and she took the doorknob in her hand and turned it. It turned easily and she gently opened the door and stared into the big room.

It was a sky-lit, attic room with white walls and hardly any furniture. An easel stood in the middle of the room with a canvas on it. And there were canvases hung on all the walls and even some stacked against the baseboards of the room. In a far corner of the room, standing leaning on his crutches and facing her with a mixture of anger and surprise, was the missing David!

She stepped into the room, going toward him. "David!" she cried.

"Why have you followed me up here?" his voice was taut.

"I was worried about you!" she said, standing in the middle of the room only a short distance from him. She now noted that the room was lighted by a hanging chandelier that dropped down from the roof not far from the skylight. It gave most of its light to the area of the room where the easel stood, leaving the corners somewhat in shadow.

"You had no right to spy on me and follow me!" was his protest.

"I was only concerned about you," she said. "You didn't tell me you could walk about on your crutches!"

"Well, now you know! And you'll tell the others!"

"Not if you don't want me to."

"You say that," he jeered, his weight slung forward on the shining, chrome crutches as he glared at her.

"I mean it!"

"No!"

"I do!" she insisted.

"This was my mother's private place," the boy said. "You shouldn't be here!"

191

"I mean no harm," she told him. "I admire her paintings." She glanced about her at the display on the walls. "And some of the best of them are up here!"

"My mother had a wonderful talent!"

"No one denies that," she said.

David came forward to her on his crutches, and she was astounded at how agile he was in using them. He said, "I don't want you to tell my father or anyone else that you found me up here."

"I won't," she said, "if that's what you want. You handle those crutches very well. I'm pleased!"

He gave her a kind of sneering look. "I can go anywhere on them. But they don't know it, and I don't mean them to."

She said, "That can only mean your paralysis isn't as bad as it was."

"It isn't," he said.

She gave him a despairing look. "But why keep it a secret?"

"That's my affair!"

"Your father would be so pleased if he only knew," she said. "You have no idea how unhappy he is because he believes you're permanently crippled."

"Let him suffer," David said. "It was his carelessness that cost me the use of my legs."

"Your mother pounded that into you," she said. "But it isn't altogether true."

"Don't say anything against my mother!" the boy told her in a warning tone.

"I didn't mean to talk against her," she said. "I think she was heartbroken, and in her distress she placed too much blame on your father."

His young face was twisted with scorn. "You'd be bound to be on his side as his new wife."

"I'm trying to be completely fair," she assured him.

"My mother was right. And I'll tell them about my legs being better when the time comes," the lad said. "The time hasn't come yet!"

"All right," she said. "I'll give you my word I'll say nothing to them. Not even to your father."

David hunched on his crutches and eyed her with suspicion. "I'm not sure I can trust you."

"You can."

He seemed to consider this for a moment before he started to move forward on his crutches. He said, "Come look at this canvas on the easel."

She followed him around to the other side of the easel where she had a full view of the painting mounted there. It was another of Sheila's landscapes of the surrounding countryside, this one a sunset study. Apparently she had been working on it at the time of her death. The entire scene was roughly sketched in and part of it was completed. The palette and paints still sat on the shelf of the easel.

She said, "It's an interesting painting."

"More interesting than you think," he said.

There was something in his tone that sent a chill down her spine. She gave the boy a quick glance and said, "Really?"

"Yes."

She studied the painting again and saw nothing all that unusual about it, so she said, "You mean because it hasn't been completed?"

There was an almost gloating smile on David's face as he informed her, "Because it is being completed."

Her eyebrows rose and she had that eerie feeling once again. "Being completed?"

"Yes."

"By whom?"

"By my mother, who else?" David demanded impatiently.

She stared at him, deciding that he must either be insane or he was deliberately playing some game on her. But as she studied him she realized that neither of these things was likely. The youth really believed what he had told her. It was written there on his face, so like the handsome face of her husband.

She gasped. "By your mother?"

"She comes and finishes it a little at a time," David said, giving his attention to the painting. "When she died there was only a small corner of it done. Since then it has been gradually added to."

"I can't believe that!" she protested.

"I have seen it happen," the boy said solemnly. "Each time I come back here I find some detail added to the painting by her ghostly hand. Soon it will all be done."

"That's a fantastic story!" Lucy protested.

The youth on the crutches said, "It's the truth!"

She said, "Someone else must come up here and work on the painting. Your father has a key. And he comes up here."

"He can't paint!" David said with derision. "He doesn't even know how to handle a brush. The work on that canvas is my mother's work."

"No. Someone else must be doing it. Someone else must also have a key!"

"There were only two keys," David said. "My mother gave me one. She had the other one herself. Father has it now. There are no other keys."

She glanced at the painting in despair. "There has to be some sort of explanation!"

"There is a simple one. My mother's ghost still works here. Just as her spirit still remains in this house. I told you that."

"You really believe it, don't you?" she said, gazing at him in wide-eyed awe.

"I do," he said. "Just as I believe my mother will avenge all the wrongs that have taken place here. I have to believe in something! Why not in my mother's ghost?"

She shook her head in despair. "I'm afraid for you."

"You needn't be."

"Some people would say you were mad!" she warned him.

"I don't tell what I think to everyone. I've told you because you've insisted that I can trust you. But if you betray me, count on my mother's ghost settling with you."

"Let's not talk so much of ghosts," she pleaded.

"Mother's phantom has been seen. Ask some of the servants."

She listened to him with a dull feeling of desperation. She knew that Mabel had also claimed to have seen the phantom and she had seen it herself. But she wouldn't go into that now. The boy was in a tense enough state.

She said, "Your father locks himself in here at times. Why?"

"Guilt."

"Why guilt?"

"Because he was not kind enough to my mother."

She said, "Couldn't it be because he loved her dearly and still misses her?"

David looked uncertain. "I don't think so."

"He must have seen the changes in the painting too," she suddenly realized. "And he must be thinking the same thing that you are. He must believe that your mother's ghost is coming here and finishing that painting."

"Why not?" the boy said with a savage satisfaction.

"It isn't right!"

"Take a good look at the painting," David said. "One day I'll have you come up here with me again. And you'll see that she has done more work on it."

Lucy found herself staring at the painting again and taking in all the detail. She finally turned to the boy on the crutches and said, "I'll know if any changes are made."

"There will be," he said. "My mother will see to that. Now I want you to leave, and I'll be coming back down shortly."

She hesitated, "Are you sure you can manage the stairs?"

"I've done it often enough before," he said defiantly. "Why not now?"

"All right," she said. And she left him standing by the easel as she went to the dark stairway and started down.

She went directly to her own room, where she paced back and forth in restless fashion and at the same time tried to straighten it all out in her mind. Discovering that David could manage so well on the crutches was a distinct surprise. This would have been enough, but her finding him upstairs in that mysterious, locked studio added to the bizarre business.

And weirdest of all was his contention that his mother's ghost was active in the house and had proved this by actually completing a good portion of the painting that she'd begun at the time of her accidental death. Further, he had claimed,

Sheila's ghost would complete the painting and avenge herself on those who had been unfair to her.

Lucy tried as best she could and still found herself unable to come up with a satisfactory explanation of the ghost painting. As for the rest of it, she was almost equally baffled. She had given her word to the boy that she would tell none of this to his father. But her promise was bound to make her feel guilty and perhaps involve her in some embarrassment.

She thought she heard David descending the stairway on his crutches, and went to the door and put her ear to it. A few minutes later she heard the sound of his crutches as he swung himself down the hall in the direction of his own room. The fact that he could get around with such dexterity was the one good side of all that had been revealed to her.

Now it was plain to her that David was possessed of a depth of which she'd not been aware. He was clever without seeming so, and wise beyond his years. The only trouble was that all his good qualities were marred by his bitterness.

She remained in her room for the balance of the evening. At various times she checked the window and saw that it was still snowing lazily outside. But there was no wind, and so the old lodge did not moan and creak as it did when there was a strong blow.

It was fairly late when she heard footsteps in the hall outside her door, and then the door opened and Charles came in. He gave her a look of mild surprise and said, "I thought you might be in bed. We worked later than we expected."

"No. I thought I'd wait for you," she said.

He came over to her, walking with the cane. Studying her closely, he said, "You look pale."

"Do I?"

"Yes," he said, his handsome face showing worry. "Is there anything wrong?"

She shook her head. "Nothing in particular. I become nervous when I'm here alone."

"Oh?"

"I'm sure it's silly of me," she went on. "But somehow I can't help it. Perhaps it's because I've heard those stories from Mabel and some of the servants."

"What stories?"

She gave him a shocked look. "You must have heard them!" She was trying to find out if he believed in the ghostly Sheila and if he thought she was finishing that painting in the upper room.

"Go on!" he urged her.

Hesitantly she said, "They say that Sheila's ghost comes back here. And you know I've seen strange shadows several times."

"Imagination!"

She was staring at him, noting the torment showing on his handsome face. "You are sure! You don't believe in Sheila's ghost?"

"No!" he said almost harshly. "No!" But she could tell that he was lying to her and that when he sequestered himself up in that lonely attic studio he believed he was close to the presence of the dead Sheila.

Chapter Eight

The next morning was a busy one at the lodge. Mabel returned from her visit to Montreal in a buoyant, good mood, and as soon as the plane was prepared, Charles left on his short visit to New York. Lucy had spent a restless night, but she had not broken her word to young David. She had kept his secret. And she was now seeing the people in the old mansion with rather different eyes.

Mabel came down in midmorning to show her a new dress that she'd purchased. An expensive brown knit with a revealing top. She paraded in it with a childish air of delight.

"How do you like it?" she asked.

Lucy smiled thinly. "It's a lovely dress, but you won't get much chance to wear it here."

The blonde rolled her eyes. "I'll find an opportunity. Before John Rhode became so strange he used to come over for dinner and we all dressed up."

"He says he's willing to come again if he's invited," she told the blonde girl.

"Then do invite him," Mabel said impulsively. "I don't care how coldly he behaves toward me. At least it will give us an excuse for company."

"I'll take care of it as soon as Charles returns," she said.

Mabel draped her lithe form on the arm of one of the easy chairs. "What happened while I was away?"

"Nothing much."

"That doesn't surprise me," Mabel said.

"I visited the graveyard and the mill."

"Oh?" Mabel showed interest.

"I had a long talk with Ned."

"Did you?" Mabel said coolly. It seemed plain that she wasn't too pleased at her husband and Lucy becoming friendly.

"Yes," she said. "And he told me something that I find surprising."

"Really?"

"He claimed that you and David had once been close. That the boy had a kind of crush on you."

Mabel eyed her uneasily. "I suppose he did. What about it?"

"You don't ever talk with him now."

"That is not my fault."

"Oh?"

"David was hateful to me. He's a cruel boy. I can't think what kind of man he'll grow into."

"I've found him rather charming in a forlorn way," she said. "Of course I don't know him well."

"That's it," the blonde told her. "Wait until you know him better."

"Lately he's been friendly with me."

"He's leading you on," Mabel warned her. "And when you are convinced you've won him over, he'll turn on you. I know! It happened with me."

She said, "But that was about the time his mother died. Don't you think that had something to do with it? That he was badly hurt?"

"No," Mabel said. "I think he's spoiled and bad-tempered. I don't intend to have anything more to do with him."

"That's too bad," she said. "I feel he needs all the help we can give him."

"Why cater to him? He only looks on it as weakness," Mabel said.

"Perhaps you're right," she said with a sigh.

"I know I'm right," Mabel said, rising. "How do you make out with Ben Huggard?"

Her question had a strange effect on

Mabel. The blonde opened her eyes wide and said, "Why do you ask me that?"

"I wondered if you had trouble with him. I've found him so terribly overbearing."

Mabel curled her lush lips. "That's because you don't know how to manage him."

"How does one manage an arrogant employee?"

"By making sure he knows he is an employee," Mabel told her. "Be sure to keep him in his place."

She nodded. "It seems to me I remember his saying that you were arrogant. And at the time I was thinking it the best word to describe him."

Mabel moved on to the right stairway. She said, "I treat him as if he were dirt. It's the only way."

"But you both grew up here together," she said. "Isn't that hard to do?"

"He was never anything to me," Mabel said. And she seemed to suddenly change her mind about the stairs. She crossed over to the left side.

"He must keep his place with Charles and Ned or they'd let him go," she said.

"I'm sure he does," Mabel said. "He's foxy! He knows just how far to go. And he tries most of his smart business with us."

And she went on up the stairs.

The morning went by without any event. And she decided to go for a stroll in the bright February sun. But first she went down to the wireless room to see David. He was seated at the ham radio as usual, sending and receiving calls. The room was filled with the sound of it. She went in and walked over by the bench so he could see her. The result was instant. He smiled, and after a moment ended his calls and shut off the wireless.

"Good afternoon," he said.

"I'm going for a walk in the snow," she said.

"Sounds fun."

"You should try it some day."

He gave her a sharp look. "You're not being serious about that, are you? You haven't told any of them?"

"No."

"I believe you," he said. "I don't suppose I ought to, but I do."

"Thank you," she said. "I didn't say a word."

David smiled grimly. "That must have taken some will power."

"It did."

"You'll be glad you kept silent," he assured her.

"I did ask your father if he believed in your mother's ghost, without saying anything about you or that upper room."

The youth in the wheelchair showed interest. "And what did he say?"

"He became very upset."

"I'll bet," David said in a gloating tone.

She frowned. "I don't think you should enjoy his torment."

"I do."

She said, "I know. But it isn't right. He loves you. I'm positive of it."

"Not interested," David said coldly. "What did he say about my mother's ghost?"

"He said it was nonsense."

"I'd expect that," David said quietly.

She gave him a knowing look. "But I'm sure he believes in the ghost in spite of the protests he made."

David nodded. "Of course he does."

"And the ghost painting," she said. "Otherwise why does he lock himself up there in that room?"

"A good question. You should ask him."

She smiled bitterly. "How I'd like to, but I can't unless I give away the fact that you had me up in that room."

"I forgot," he said. "Too bad."

She said, "Mabel is home."

"That also doesn't interest me," David said with a look of disgust.

"She's in great humor and has some new dresses."

"No doubt."

"She claims that you are cruel and spoiled."

"I don't mind that at all," he said. "Just so long as I'm not her friend."

"I'm sure that bothers her."

"Let it," he said.

"She wants to have a dinner party and try and get your uncle John Rhode to attend."

David looked gloomy at this. "Uncle John is a good sort. I hope he doesn't come. He hasn't been here since my mother's death."

"I know," she said. "But at least he ought to come and visit you."

David showed a boyish forlornness. "I miss seeing him, but there are things you have to put up with."

"I think you enjoying punishing yourself," she suggested.

"Maybe," he said with a sudden wry grin. "There are certain benefits about keeping to myself up here."

"I'm sure of that," she said.

"And thanks for saying nothing about

last night," the youth in the wheelchair said. "It's important to me that none of the others know."

She left him busy at the wireless again and went downstairs and outside. She walked toward the village and wasn't long on her way when she heard the sound of a car behind her. It came to a halt on the road beside her, and she saw that it was John Rhode driving a Jeep station wagon.

John Rhode put down the window of the wagon and said, "Can I give you a lift?"

She smiled at him. "I'm not going anywhere."

"Neither am I," he said. "I have the afternoon off. I'll take you for a drive."

"All right," she said. "Since you have the time." And she went around and got in the other side.

He gave her a good-humored glance as she seated herself beside him. "You like the outdoors, it seems."

She sighed. "I sometimes find the lodge too confining. I feel I have to get away from it."

The gaunt-faced young man at the wheel nodded as he drove on toward the village. "I understand. I get that same feeling some days at the mill office."

"Charles and Ned always seem to have

so much work," she said. "How do you happen to be able to take afternoons off?"

"I'm not an important member of the firm," he said with a smile. "That has some advantages. I like to be free a part of the time."

"I'd say you were fortunate."

"Charles is in New York today, isn't he?" John Rhode said as they drove by the tall, gray mill buildings.

"Yes. He'll be back some time early to-morrow."

"Mabel is back."

"Yes, with a wardrobe of new dresses that she is anxious to show off. She even suggested that I have you to dinner so she could dress up."

"Why not?" he said in joking fashion.

"Would you like to come?"

"Anything to make the lovely Mabel happy," he said.

"Then I'll make the invitation official," she told him. "Cocktails at seven with dinner following."

"I'll be there."

"And do please go up and visit with David for a little," she begged him. "I know he's missed seeing you."

"I will," the man at the wheel said as they drove along a wooded road on the other side of the village. "How is he?"

"I don't know," she said. "There are times I worry about him. I think he should get out more."

"I'd be willing to take him for a drive any day," John Rhode said.

"The problem is to get him interested in leaving the house. Did he take part in many outdoor activities before his accident?"

John Rhode had his eyes on the winding road as he said, "Yes. He used to skate, ski, and toboggan."

She gave the gaunt John an excited glance. "Toboggan! I hadn't thought about that. Couldn't he still do that if he had others with him?"

"I suppose so."

"I must talk to him about it."

John smiled grimly. "I'd say you have a lot of persuading to do. He won't even go down to the dinner table or take a ride in a car."

"The idea of tobogganing again might appeal to him."

"It could be worth a try," the man at the wheel admitted. "But I wouldn't count on anything."

"I know that," she said with a sigh as she gazed out at the snow-mantled trees lining the road.

A moment or two later they came up on a rise to an open area overlooking a river. There was a tiny wharf by the cleared parking space and a dozen or so wooden huts set out on the ice near the wharf. The river was fairly wide, with hills in the background. John turned off the motor of the station wagon and gave her a friendly look.

"This is where I often drive," he said. "Let's get out and stretch our legs."

"I'd love to," she said enthusiastically. "I've never been this far before. I didn't know you had a river of this size near the village."

"One of the benefits," he said. "In the spring we have log drives from up in the hills and bring a lot of lumber down this way."

They got out of the jeep and walked down to the wharf. He explained that the huts set out on the ice were used by fishermen for protection. They stayed in the huts and fished through holes in the ice.

As they stood on the wharf, two skidoos came racing along past them to vanish in roaring indifference around the bend in the river. John Rhode shook his head grimly.

"Those things are a mixed blessing," he said in a tone of annoyance. "They make getting around easier under certain conditions, but people tend to abuse them."

"They make such a roar," she said. "No more peaceful forests."

"I know some of the villagers chase animals with them, and they have no respect for property. They come across my fields any time of the day or night they like."

"I've heard them," she recalled. "But never very close to the lodge."

John studied the shining ice of the river. "When I was a boy we used to come down here and watch horses and sleighs in ice races. There was some beauty and sport to that. Now all we have are these noisy, ugly machines."

She smiled at him. "I suppose every generation complains about the changes that come along and clings to its own good memories of the past."

John shot her a sharp glance. "You surely don't believe that all change is for the better?"

"No, I guess not," she said.

He said, "I'd better stop complaining. The first sign of old age must be to regret change."

Lucy said, "No one could call you old."

"Older than you," John Rhode said, giving her a teasing look. "And so is Charles, for that matter."

"I know."

"Let's go down and stroll along the ice," he suggested. "I can show you more of the country from down there."

She was quite agreeable to the idea, so they clambered down the wooden ladder built on the side of the wharf and made their way across the ice to the middle of the river. From there you could see far up and down its wide expanse.

Strolling along slowly, John asked her, "How are things at Seven Timbers?"

"About the same."

"And Charles?"

"He still baffles me," she said with a slight frown. "But I'm sure of one thing."

"What?"

"He believes that Sheila's ghost comes back."

The gaunt young man eyed her sharply. "Why do you say that?"

"Because of the way he acts and what he has said when I've questioned him about it."

"What are your feelings?"

"I was a skeptic in the beginning. Now I'm starting to feel that he and the others may be right. I've had some strange experiences myself."

John looked thoughtful as they continued their slow walk. He said, "Which brings us back to Sheila's death from that mysterious fall on the stairway."

"Yes."

"I'm still not satisfied with the facts we have," he said.

"I don't blame you. Ned is very worried about Charles. He is afraid he may be on the edge of a nervous breakdown."

"Pressure of a guilty conscience, perhaps," was John Rhode's comment.

She gave the man at her side an anxious glance. "You still believe Charles may have been responsible?"

"Yes. But that theory has to be repulsive to you."

"I love Charles," she agreed. "I have to believe in him."

"But you admit he has behaved strangely."

"Yes."

"So you could be wrong about him."

"I don't want to be," she said.

"I can understand that," John Rhode said. "And I hope for your sake I'm wrong."

She sighed. "There are times when I feel David knows more than he will say. That he has locked himself up in that wireless room because of it."

"What could he know?"

"I haven't any idea," she admitted. "But he talks rather wildly about his mother's ghost returning and about her avenging herself on her enemies."

John halted and stared at her. "The boy said that?"

"Yes."

"Interesting."

"Perhaps if you talked with him," she suggested.

"I'll try when I come over tonight," he said, as they resumed walking. "I see now that I made a mistake avoiding the house."

"I'm sure of that."

"I was very shattered by my sister's sudden death," he said. "Not until you arrived did I feel able to cope with things over there."

"Really?"

"Yes," he said. "I think you may be in the same danger as Sheila, and I want to try to save you."

"Thanks," she said. "But I don't know why anyone would want to kill me."

"That's something to find out," he said. "We may be dealing with a madman. In that case a motive doesn't have to be logical."

"I hadn't thought of that."

"It's an important possibility," John Rhode said. "You say you've found Ned pleasant?"

"Yes."

"I think he hides his true self a lot," the man at her side observed. "And I'm sure he worries a lot about his wife."

"Mabel is a problem for him," she agreed.

"I don't think all those trips she makes on her own are for clothes alone."

She said, "Ben Huggard hinted that."

"He should know."

"From what he said she is meeting some man or men. But then he's such an unpleasant character I doubt whether you can pay serious attention to anything he says."

"You can in this instance," John told her. "He dislikes all of us who own the mill. So he'll do anything he can against us. His father was killed in a mill accident years ago, and he has never forgiven the Prentiss family."

"Mabel isn't a Prentiss," she pointed out.

"She married one," John said. "That makes her a natural enemy."

"If he harbors those kind of hatreds, he

must be a little mad," she said.

"An interesting possibility," the gaunt-faced John agreed. "Are you cold?"

She glanced up at the sky, which had clouded over, and said, "The sun has gone and I am beginning to feel a little chilly."

He smiled at her. "Time to go back."

She halted and turned to make the return journey to the wharf. Gazing up at his serious face, she said, "This has been fun!"

"I've enjoyed it a lot," John said. And at the same time he took her completely by surprise by suddenly drawing her to him and kissing her. The kiss was a brief one, and he quickly released her, with his face showing a guilty expression. "Sorry! I didn't mean that to happen!"

She stared at him. "But it happened!"

"Impulse," he said. "My error."

"I am Charles' wife," she reminded him.

"I won't forget it again," he assured her.

They walked the rest of the way back to the wharf in a kind of awkward silence. He helped her up the ladder to the wharf, and they strolled over to the station wagon. He opened the door and let her in, and then went around to the driver's side and slid behind the wheel. They began the drive back to the village.

She found herself filled with mixed feelings. She liked John and enjoyed being in his company. And she felt that he had really meant no harm by embracing her. Yet she didn't want it to become a pattern. So she knew a sudden show of reserve was advisable. She was mixed-up badly enough already without involving herself in a romantic affair with the stern John Rhode.

After they'd been driving a little while, he said, "I trust I'm still invited for dinner?"

"Of course."

"Thanks," he said, his eyes fixed on the road ahead.

As they neared the village she asked him some questions about the several small stores there. He drove her along the short main street and showed them to her. He also pointed out the one tavern that the area boasted.

After they drove on, he said, "The tavern is where Ben Huggard spends a lot of his time."

"He mentioned that," she said, happy that they'd passed over the spell of embarrassment and were able to talk more or less freely again.

He said, "The Village is busier during the summer months when you can get in and out more easily by road."

"Right now you depend on the plane and the train service," she said.

"The roads are barely passable," he explained. "But when you reach the adjoining villages you still are a long way from anywhere."

"Are they smaller than Seven Timbers?"

John nodded. "Yes. Our doctor serves them, so he spends a day or two a week outside this village."

"And he is a company doctor?"

"That's right. The only way you can get a medical man to stay here is to guarantee him a regular wage. The mill does that, and the people benefit."

"Is he an old man or a young one?" she asked.

"He's middle-aged," John Rhode said with a bleak smile. "His big problem is that he is an alcoholic. That's why he took the job here. But when he's himself he's all right."

"That's encouraging," she said. "What is his name?"

"Mason," the man at the wheel said. "Shephen Mason. You'll be bound to meet him."

John Rhode let her out at the front door of the mansion, and she left him with the understanding that he would come to dinner as they'd planned. It seemed that they'd managed to put the incident on the river behind them and returned to their pleasant, casual friendship.

Mabel was seated by the fireplace, reading, when Lucy came in. She gave her a searching glance and said, "You've been out a good long while."

"I met John Rhode," she said.

"Oh?" Mabel's blonde loveliness was all at once frigid.

She smiled to reassure the other girl. "I did what you asked. I suggested he join us at dinner tonight. Now you have a chance to dress for the occasion."

The blonde's pretty face relaxed in a smile. "Did you truly?"

"Yes, just now."

"And he really accepted? I'm surprised. It's the first time he's been here since Sheila's death."

"I think he's over that," she said. "We drove to the river and walked on the ice for a while."

Mabel's eyebrows lifted. "Sounds romantic!"

She blushed, since this brought back remembrance of what had happened. She quickly said, "It was too cold to be romantic, but I enjoyed it."

Mabel got up, "I'll tell Mrs. Warren we'll have an extra person for dinner and to prepare something special. It's too bad Charles won't be home."

"He won't mind," she said. "And, we can have John in again when Charles is home."

"Yes, I suppose so," the blonde said. "Since he is going to visit us again."

The rest of the day went by without further event. Ned was mildly surprised to hear that John was coming to dinner but he at once agreed it was a good thing.

Frowning, he said, "It has been difficult since Sheila's death. He has avoided us socially, and yet we've been constantly exposed to each other at the office."

Lucy said, "He took her death hard."

"Without a question," Ned said. "But I could never see why he should blame us."

"Sorrow expresses itself in strange ways," she suggested.

At seven Mabel came downstairs in an exciting green velvet creation with a deep, plunging neckline. Lucy wore her expensive gold knit dress, which was a favorite, and Ned cooperated by donning black tie and jacket. When John Rhode arrived he was also in a tuxedo. They made a rather handsome group standing before the fire-place and having their drinks.

Lucy took John aside for a moment and said, "Why don't you go up and see David before dinner?"

"Have I time?" he asked.

"Yes. Mabel has asked Mrs. Warren to serve us at eight-thirty," she said. "I know he'd appreciate seeing you."

"I'll go up then," John said with a thin smile. And he left them to pay a visit to the invalid youth.

Mabel was a trifle upset at his deserting them. "He could have gone up there later," she pouted prettily over her drink.

"I told him to go now," she said. "Other-wise David might think he only came to see him as an afterthought."

Ned nodded his agreement. "I think your idea smart," he said. "Especially since David is so oversensitive."

Mabel said, "Then why do we all cater to him so? We only spoil him more!"

Ned gave her a reproving look. "Just be-cause your experience with him was bad, don't expect the rest of us to turn our backs on him."

Lucy said, "He is so lonely and mixed-up."

Mabel took a sip of her drink and said

somewhat tartly, "I'll go along with the mixed-up."

John Rhode came down to rejoin them after about ten minutes, and the situation eased. Lucy asked if he'd had a good chat with David, and he said that he had, but he didn't elaborate on that. They enjoyed the blazing log fire for a little longer and then went in to dinner.

Mrs. Warren had done well. From the candlelit table to the excellent roast beef, everything was excellent. And when it came to the end of the meal, they were all served with a mouth-watering lot of individual strawberry shortcakes. As they lingered over coffee and brandy afterwards, Mabel offered a revelation.

"Weren't those shortcakes good?" she said as an opener.

"Excellent," John Rhode said. "The berries seemed almost fresh, but of course they had to be frozen."

Mabel smiled. "They were made into shortcakes, and the cakes frozen within an hour or two after the berries were picked. That is why they have such a fine flavor."

Ned said, "We used to have shortcake often. But this is the first time in a long while."

The lovely Mabel gave her husband a

wise smile. "And do you know why? It's because it was Sheila who always made the shortcakes. It was a favorite thing with her."

Ned frowned slightly. "I guess you're right."

"I know I am," she said. "As a matter of fact, Sheila made the shortcakes you've just had tonight!"

John Rhode put down his coffee cup and stared at her. "You must be joking." And he sounded as if he felt the joke wasn't in the best of taste.

"No," Mabel said triumphantly. "Sheila did make the shortcakes. She did a whole lot of them shortly before her accident. We put them in the freezer. And there are still about two dozen of them left. I brought out the ones we had tonight in honor of the occasion."

"That's very interesting," Lucy said quietly. She felt a little strange at the idea of having just finished eating a dish prepared by her dead predecessor, but she realized that Mabel had done it in an effort to please John.

Ned also seemed to have the same idea. He said, "Well, it seems that Sheila's influence still prevails in more than her paintings. The dessert was excellent, and I'm sure she would like to know that we enjoyed it."

"Yes," John Rhode said dryly.

Lucy could tell that he wasn't pleased, and she quickly turned the conversation to a discussion about the sleigh rides on the river and the abominable era that the skidoos had brought in. This at least stirred up enough indignation to take their minds off the business of the shortcakes.

But John Rhode did not regain his easy good humor for the rest of the evening. And when he left rather early, she had the distinct impression that he was upset. When she returned to join Ned and Mabel by the living-room fireplace, she found they were both of the same opinion.

Ned said, "I think serving those shortcakes offended John."

Mabel shook her head and said plaintively, "I can't think why. I expected him to be pleased."

"I even felt a little odd about it," Ned said. "It was as if Sheila's ghost had prepared the dessert. I think it was a mistake. You could have served the cakes without mentioning anything about them."

"But the whole point was that Sheila had prepared them!" an upset Mabel exclaimed. "Mrs. Warren didn't seem to

226

think there was anything wrong with the idea."

Ned said impatiently, "You know she wouldn't argue with you about anything!"

"Everything is always blamed on me!" Mabel said indignantly and left them, mounting the left stairway in a sulky mood.

Ned turned to Lucy and apologized, "Sorry. I'm afraid we made a mess of your night."

"I don't think we should worry about it," she said.

"Probably not," Ned agreed. He bade her goodnight and left.

She then went on to her own bedroom. She was tempted to stop by and see David for a moment, but since it was late she decided not to. She could ask him about his conversation with his uncle in the morning. In the bedroom she slowly changed into her night things.

After she was in bed and had turned the light out, she thought she heard David making his way along the corridor by her door on his crutches. She listened and the sounds faded. She wasn't sure but she felt that he probably was on his way to the attic studio and the ghostly paintings.

Then she fell asleep, and it was not until some time later that she awoke suddenly to stare up into the darkness of her bedroom with a feeling of distress. She was certain she heard the door of her room slowly opening!

Chapter Nine

The door from the corridor slowly creaked open, and to her complete horror she knew that someone had come into the bedroom. She tried to cry out but couldn't! Literally paralyzed by fear, she lay there in the darkness listening to the ghostly footsteps and rustlings, unable to do anything about it.

It seemed that the room was filled with an icy chill related to the supernatural. She tried to penetrate the darkness with her terrified eyes, but she could see nothing. Yet she knew there was a presence there slowly moving about. And then she heard the door slowly close again, and the ordeal was over!

But was it? She tried to raise herself in bed and found that she was deathly weak and perspiring in a wild fashion. With a moan she made another effort to lift herself from the pillow, and this time succeeded. Now she realized how ill she was. Her head was reeling and she was alternately hot and chilled. She waited for a moment and then somehow rose from her bed and, groping her way through the darkness, staggered to the door.

She leaned against it for a moment, thinking that she might collapse. Then she summoned all her remaining will to open the door and stumbled out into the hallway. Once out there she lifted her voice weakly in appeals for help. Leaning against the wall as she waited for someone who might have heard her to come, she tried to think clearly — but it was useless. Her mind was a blur.

Next someone came hurrying to her in the semidarkness of the hall, and she heard the prim Mrs. Warren exclaim, "Mrs. Prentiss! What is it?"

It was then that she turned to the older woman and tried to speak. But she merely moved her lips and silently collapsed.

When she came to, it was daylight and she was in her bed. A tall, white-haired man with a bloated red face was bending over her. She had never seen him before, but he appeared to be regarding her with some concern.

"Can you hear me, Mrs. Prentiss?" he asked.

She stared up at him, then weakly said, "Yes."

"Good," he said, "I'm Dr. Mason. You've been a very ill young woman."

Slowly remembrance returned to her. "What?" she asked vaguely.

"Don't worry yourself now," he said. "I'm going to give you something to make you sleep in a few minutes."

The fear she'd known came back to her, and she tried to lift herself up as she protested, "No!"

He eased her back with his hands and said, "I don't want you thrashing about for a little. You mustn't panic!"

"Tell me?" she begged him.

"What has happened?" he said. "I'll do the best I can. You somehow were poisoned. I had to pump your stomach out, and it's lucky I got to you in time. A few hours more and the poison would have done its work."

"How?" she asked.

"I haven't found out yet," he said. "We're getting too many food-poisoning cases these days. You may have just been unlucky enough to have gotten hold of some tainted food, or it may even have been from some virus. The main thing is that the crisis is over and you're recovering."

"I don't understand," she said.

"Nor do I," the doctor was willing to admit.

"The others?" she questioned him.

"Are all right," he assured her. "It appears you were the only unlucky one."

As he finished speaking, the door opened and a distraught-looking Charles came striding into the room with an air of urgency. He came to her bedside and stood there across from the doctor.

Bending to kiss her forehead, he said, "I've only just come back. I heard what happened."

She smiled wanly. "The doctor says I'll be all right."

Holding one of her small hands in his, he straightened up and asked the doctor, "Is that so?"

"Yes. We've got rid of the poison."

"What poison?" Charles demanded sternly.

"I haven't any idea," the white-haired Dr. Mason said.

"No idea?" Charles asked incredulously.

"I'm afraid that's the story," Dr. Stephen Mason said in an apologetic tone. "But I do know she either had bad food or it was some sort of bug."

"I see," Charles said in a grim tone. "Well, at least that narrows it down some."

"She had a very near call," the doctor said. "But now what she needs is rest. I'd say a sedative to give her eight hours or more sleep. Then she should be all right."

"Later," she said. "Not yet. Let me talk with my husband first."

"I'll leave the medicine," Dr. Mason said. "You can take it when you like. I'll drop by and see you tomorrow morning." And he picked up his black medicine bag from the chair by her bedside and opened it.

Charles questioned the doctor in a worried voice, "Will she need a nurse?"

Dr. Mason handed him a small brown bottle and shook his head. "No. I think not."

"What about the medicine?" he asked.

"You can give it to her. The dosage is on the bottle," the doctor said.

"And after that she's just to sleep?"

"As long as she can," Dr. Mason said. "When she wakens she will feel better."

Charles held the medicine bottle nervously. "You don't think there should be anyone watching her?"

"You can have someone at her bedside part of the time, if it will make you feel better," Dr. Mason said. "But she doesn't require skilled help."

"I see," Charles said doubtfully. "I'll be with her a part of the time, and perhaps my sister-in-law or one of the maids."

Dr. Mason nodded. "Anyone." He turned to tell her, "I'll see you in the morning again, Mrs. Prentiss."

"Thank you," she said faintly.

"You've come through it very well," the doctor said in parting.

As soon as she and Charles were alone in the room, he put the medicine bottle on the bedside table and sat on the edge of her bed. His handsome face had a worn look.

"I didn't expect to come home to anything like this!"

"Sorry."

"Not your fault," he said. "I'm only thankful it's no worse. When did it first hit you?"

"In the night. Probably after midnight."

"Tell me about it," he urged her.

She closed her eyes and tried to collect her thoughts. And then it gradually came back to her and she said, "I was awakened by the door opening!"

"The door to this room?"

"Yes. I was terrified. And I was also deathly ill, though I didn't realize it then. I sensed someone coming into the room and

234

moving around. I felt it to be a ghostly presence."

"Please," he said, "none of that."

She gazed up at him earnestly. "It's true. I wasn't able to see anything. And after a little the door closed, and I knew that whoever had been here had gone."

"I'll ask about it," her husband said. "It may have been Mrs. Warren."

"Why should she come in here? And it wasn't her in any case."

"Then what?"

"I began to understand how ill I was. I had a dreadful time getting out of bed and reaching the hall to call for help. But somehow I managed it. Mrs. Warren heard me and came out to see what was wrong."

"And then the doctor was called?"

"I don't know," she said. "You'll have to ask Mabel or Ned. I collapsed. I don't remember anything after that."

"It's puzzling," Charles said worriedly. "What could it have been?"

"We had a special dinner last night. John Rhode came to dine with us."

Charles registered surprise. "That was unusual."

"It's a long story," she said. "But anyway, he came."

"And?"

She suddenly remembered something and stared up at him in dismay. She said, "We had a special dessert. Strawberry shortcakes that Sheila made before her death and put in the freezer to keep."

Her husband's handsome face became more drawn. "Shortcakes made by Sheila?"

"Yes," she said. "Mabel made a point of mentioning it at the table. And I'm sure it upset John."

Charles frowned. "Not much wonder. That was tactless of Mabel."

A new thought had come to her and she gazed at him with frightened eyes. "Perhaps it was the strawberry shortcake! Could it be that Sheila meant me to be ill?"

"Are you suggesting that a ghost poisoned you?"

"I don't know what to think."

"If the shortcake made you ill, it was because it had gone bad in some way. Possibly during the time it was in the freezer. Mabel should have thrown all that stuff away long ago!"

She said, "It must have been the shortcake."

"None of the others have been ill," he reminded her.

"They were made in individual servings," she said. "Mine could have been the only tainted one."

Charles sighed. "We'll think about that later. Just now I'll give you your medicine and you'll get the sleep you need."

"I don't feel I need sleep," she protested.

"I'm sure you do," he said firmly.

He filled a glass with water and gave her the medicine, then sat by her bedside for it to take effect. She watched him as she waited for the medicine to make her sleepy, and she thought he looked more weary than before he'd left.

She asked him, "How was your trip?"

"All right."

"Did you do anything about David? Did you talk to a psychiatrist about him?"

Charles frowned. "Don't worry about David now. We want to get you better."

"Tell me!" she insisted. "Did you do anything?"

"I talked to one fellow," her husband said. "But I didn't get very far. He said he'd have to see David and talk to him before he could make any suggestions."

"That is what you should do," she said, beginning to feel a wave of sleepiness.

"I told him I'd let him know when he could come here," Charles said.

Her eyes were closing and she was confusedly trying to make some sense of it all. Everyone in the house believed in the existence of Sheila's ghost. Even Charles, though he continued to deny it. And David had shown her the ghost painting that went on in that attic studio. If Sheila could return from the grave to work on a painting, why couldn't she return and put some sort of poison in the shortcake? If you accepted one, why not the other?

As she reached this point in her reasoning, sleep took over. And when she wakened again it was evening and Mabel was seated at her bedside, reading. When the blonde girl saw she was awake, she put aside her book.

"What time is it?" she asked Mabel in a somewhat stronger voice than before.

"Eight o'clock in the evening," Mabel said. "It's dark. You slept right through the day."

She sat up in bed. "I do feel better."

"Would you like something to eat? The doctor said you could have consommé or anything light."

Lucy nodded. "Yes, I'd like some consommé."

"I'll go let Mrs. Warren know," the blonde girl said, rising. "You gave us a terrible fright."

"I'm sorry."

Mabel's pretty face twisted in a grimace. "And now Charles is blaming me."

"Blaming you?"

"Yes. He claims if I'd not given you that strawberry shortcake, you'd not have been sick. I call it nonsense. We all had it."

"It doesn't matter," she said wearily. "He's upset and just has to blame somebody. Don't worry about it."

"I can't help worrying," the blonde girl said. "But the main thing is that you're better." And she went off to tell Mrs. Warren about the consommé.

Lucy's head was still a bit light, but she slowly got out of bed and went into the bathroom and had a glass of cold water. Then she stepped under the shower. The shower made her feel much more alert and well. She put on a fresh nightgown and dressing gown and fixed her hair a little. By the time Mrs. Warren came with a tray she looked almost her normal self.

Mrs. Warren eyed her from behind her heavy hornrimmed glasses as she placed the tray on the bedside table. "My goodness! You look so much better!"

She smiled wanly. "I feel better."

"Are you supposed to be out of bed?" the housekeeper worried.

"I'm sure it doesn't matter," she said. "Now it's just a question of getting my strength back."

Mrs. Warren fussed with the tray in her prim fashion. "I have some good food for you here. And a nice cup of tea. Just sit down and enjoy it."

"Thank you," she said, sitting down before the tray. It smelled most tempting.

Mrs. Warren stood by and said, "I worried when Mrs. Mabel Prentiss decided to use those shortcakes. I don't hold with keeping anything that long. And then I didn't like the idea of eating from dead hands."

She glanced up from the consommé. "It wasn't exactly that."

"Too close to it for my liking," the housekeeper said. "Mr. Charles told me this afternoon to destroy all the rest of them. And I did. No one else will be poisoned by them."

"Suppose the strawberry shortcake wasn't responsible?" she asked.

"It had to be it," the prim Mrs. Warren said firmly. "All the other food I served was fresh made. And no one was sick but you."

"That does make a pretty strong case against it," she admitted.

"It satisfied me," the older woman assured her.

She finished the light meal and Mrs. Warren took away the empty tray. Left alone Lucy felt restless, and she decided to walk down the hall and visit David. She remembered that she had thought she'd heard him making his way down the hall on his crutches the previous night. That was before everything else had happened.

She made her way to the wireless room and found him giving out his call letters. He halted when she entered the tiny room and switched the set off. There was an apprehensive look on his boyish face as he turned to her.

He said, "Close the door to the hall before we talk."

"All right," she said. And she did, and then she returned to the youth in the wheelchair. "You're being very careful tonight."

His eyes met hers, and there was a serious gleam in them. He said, "Don't you think it's about time?"

"Because of what happened to me?"

"Yes. You're lucky to be alive," he said.

"So the doctor said."

David gave her a strange look. "I told you my mother would have her revenge.

241

And I warned you that she'd send you away. So you had one of the shortcakes she made and you nearly died."

"Are you going to blame it on the ghost, too?"

"Why not?"

"I wish I could offer you some valid argument," she said wearily. "I can't."

"Uncle John came up to see me last night, and he said then he thought you were in danger," David informed her. "And it didn't take too long for it to turn out that way."

She said, "I no longer know what to believe."

David gave her a solemn look. "Better leave here."

"Do you want me to go?"

"No."

"Then why say that?" she asked.

"Because if you do remain here, I've a pretty fair hunch other things are going to happen. I don't think you'll escape alive if you don't go now."

Her eyes widened. "You think your dead mother hates me that much?"

The youth in the wheelchair shrugged. "Let us say somebody does."

"I can't leave Charles," she said.

"My father isn't worth the sacrifice,"

David said with disgust.

"I think he is."

"You're pretty stubborn," he said with a sigh.

"Yes."

"And maybe a little stupid?"

"Could be."

"You should never have married Dad in the first place," the crippled David complained. "And coming here with him was your second mistake."

"And my third?"

"Probably becoming friendly with me," David said desperately. "I can't help you, and I want to."

"If you want to I'm sure you can," she said with a smile.

"Not unless you help yourself," he warned her.

"And to do that?"

"I've already told you, get away from here as quickly as you can," David said.

She said, "I heard the ghost in my room last night."

"Didn't I tell you!"

"It came and moved about the room and left. And I thought I heard you in the hall about the same time."

David showed concern. "Don't mix me up in this!"

"I was certain I heard you."

He looked frightened. "No."

"Whatever you say," she said. "I have a plan for you when I get back on my feet."

"What?"

"How long since you've been tobogganing?"

David looked at her as if she were mad. "How long do you think?" he asked bitterly.

"You can toboggan again. I'll help you, and so will John Rhode."

The youth in the wheelchair said, "That's a laugh!"

"I mean it."

"Sure you do," he jeered. "Why not bring me up a jump rope?"

"You may not be able to walk well, but with someone with you there's no reason why you shouldn't be able to ride a toboggan. You'll be ill if you stay up here and never get any air."

"So far it seems I'm doing better than you," the boy in the chrome wheelchair said with sarcasm.

She said, "Think about it. I'll be back." And she left him.

When she reached the balcony she heard John Rhode talking to Charles in the living room. So she went up to the railing and let herself be seen. Mabel and Ned were also down there, and the blonde girl looked up and saw her.

"There she is now," Mabel said.

John had his overcoat on and fur hat in hand. He now glanced up and said, "I thought you were ill in bed."

"I was," she said. "But I'm better now." And she walked across to the right stairway and started to go down it. She'd just descended three or four steps when she somehow stumbled and with a tiny cry of fear pitched forward. She only fell a step or two, and Charles meanwhile had raced up the stairs to meet her.

"I thought you were due for a bad fall," he said in a shaken voice.

She allowed him to help her to her feet. Still leaning on him, she said, "I'll be all right."

"Better not come on down," he warned.

"I can," she insisted. "I'm not dizzy or anything like that. I think my slipper caught in the stair padding."

Charles escorted her the rest of the way down and led her to a chair. He said, "Sit there. You have to be weak, whether you admit it or not!"

She sat and realized that she still was weaker than she'd guessed. John Rhode had come to stand before her with a serious look on his face.

He said, "If you'd had a fall I'd have felt I was to blame. I didn't intend to bring you down here."

"I'm glad to see you," she said.

"Sorry you were ill," John Rhode said. "I was very upset when I heard about it."

"Thanks," she told him.

His eyes met hers, with a sort of strange look in them, as he said, "I'm told the doctor doesn't know what caused you to be ill."

"It could have been anything," she said. "A virus perhaps."

"Yes, perhaps," he said. He nodded toward the stairway. "I'd keep off those stairs until I felt better."

"Yes," she said.

"Charles lost one wife on them. I'm certain he wouldn't want to lose another that way," John Rhode said with an ironic glance at her husband.

Charles flushed. And he mumbled, "I didn't want her coming down here at all."

"My fault," John Rhode said. "I'll leave now. But I'll keep in touch with you."

"Please do!" she said with a meaningful note in her voice.

He nodded. Charles saw him out. While

this was going on Ned came over to her and said, "Since this is my first chance to talk to you since last night, let me say I'm sorry too."

She gave him a weary smile. "I'm the one who has been the nuisance. I'm sorry you had to get the doctor in the middle of the night."

"To get him sobered was the big task," Mabel said with a look of disgust on her lovely face. "You know he was soused when we called him."

Ned gave his young wife a reproachful look. He said, "Well, he came. That's the main thing."

"How could he not?" Mabel demanded. "The mill pays him a big salary for doing nothing most of the time."

Charles came back in time to halt this argument and take her upstairs. She was glad to allow him to help her, although she felt that by the morning she would have recovered a good deal more.

In the bedroom Charles saw her safely in her bed and then prepared for bed himself. He told her, "It was silly of you to risk going downstairs. You could have been badly hurt."

"I wasn't," she said.

"It was too close for comfort," he told

her. "John Rhode could have waited until tomorrow to call here."

"I don't think that mattered," she protested. "He didn't make me go down."

"His being there made you feel you should," was her husband's argument. And she could tell that he was probably angry because his one-time brother-in-law had called at all. He seemingly had no more use for John Rhode than the gaunt-faced young man had for him.

Charles settled down in bed and turned the lights out. In the darkness she lay there seeking sleep. In a very short time she could hear Charles snoring softly. And she wondered how long it would be before she was able to rest as well.

She was reviewing all that had happened that evening when all at once Charles began to stir in his bed and talk in his sleep. As usual his words were garbled, but by listening intently she heard the words "Sheila," "stairs," and, most frightening of all, "murder." Then he turned in bed and the talking ceased.

Once again she found herself convinced that her husband of a short time knew more about what was happening in the old mansion than he chose to reveal. His reference to murder in his sleep had to be the product of his thoughts. And if he were thinking of murder, it had to be Sheila's or the attempt that had been made on her.

She stared up into the darkness with frightened eyes and worried that perhaps young David might have given her the best advice of all. He had told her to leave the sinister old lodge! She fell asleep finally, debating it all in her mind.

When she awoke the sun was shining in the window and Charles was gone. She sat up and found she felt a great deal better. And she had showered and dressed by the time Mrs. Warren came up with her breakfast.

The prim woman put down the tray. "I've brought you something a little more hearty," she announced.

"Thank you," she said, sitting at the table.

The train whistle sounded far away, and Mrs. Warren went to the window to look out as it rumbled by in the distance. She said, "The morning mail and newspaper will have come on that. They always throw the mail bag off at the station."

"Is there only one mail a day?" she asked.

"Just on the morning train," Mrs. Warren confirmed, coming back from the window. "The evening train only stops and lets off passengers, if there are any. And I think it picks up mail, but it doesn't leave any."

"I see," she said, enjoying the bacon and eggs that had been prepared for her.

Mrs. Warren eyed her primly. "I think you're a wonder. To come back to health so quickly."

She smiled. "I wasn't really ill, I was poisoned."

"You were sick enough," the older woman said. "I wish you could have seen yourself that night."

"I'm satisfied to have skipped that," she said.

"I never saw Mrs. Mabel so upset," the housekeeper confided. "She kept crying and saying if only Mr. Charles were here. And of course it was Mr. Ned who had to get the doctor and everything."

"I can imagine," she said.

"Mrs. Mabel isn't any good when things go wrong," was the housekeeper's opinion.

There was a knock on the door, and when Mrs. Warren went over and opened it Dr. Stephen Mason was standing out there with his black bag in hand.

"How is my patient this morning?" he asked.

She turned in her chair with her tea cup in hand. "Just finishing my breakfast," she said with a smile.

The big man with the white hair and bloated red face came in. He had a rather pleasant face except for his eyes, which were shifty-looking.

He said, "Your condition speaks well for my doctoring."

"I couldn't agree more," Lucy said.

Mrs. Warren removed the breakfast tray and left while the doctor remained to examine her. He found her in satisfactory shape and advised her not to overdo things for a few days.

As he prepared to leave, she asked, "Have you come to any decision as to what poisoned me?"

The shifty eyes avoided any direct glance as he said, "No."

She said, "You mean it's going to be another mystery."

He frowned and said, "Another mystery?"

"Like Sheila's fall."

He showed surprise. "Oh, that!"

"Yes. It was never really explained either, was it?"

"I'd forgotten about it," he said uneasily.

She gave him a rebuking smile. "Come now, Doctor."

He said, "What has it to do with you?"

"She was married to my husband."

"Aside from that?"

"She was struck down mysteriously. And now it seems I have almost suffered a similar fate in a different way. Terribly mysterious."

The doctor's red, bloated face looked grim as he told her, "I wouldn't dwell on that if I were you."

"You think it might be bad for my peace of mind?" she said in a mocking tone.

"I think your husband's first wife tripped on the stairs and you picked up some sort of virus. I see no coincidence and no mystery in either case."

She nodded. "And I'm sure that Charles would agree with you."

The doctor looked upset. "I think he would!"

"You'll forgive me, then, if I don't," she said. "And please don't think I'm not grateful for what you've done. I am. Good morning, Doctor."

"Good morning," he said brusquely, and he hurried out as if he couldn't wait another minute.

She stood in the middle of the bedroom and thought of the way he'd reacted, and felt sure that she had frightened him. That

Dr. Stephen Mason knew a great deal more than he was letting on. And so did her husband.

She was about to leave the room when she heard another knock on the door and said, "Come in."

This time it was Mabel. The blonde was wearing a chic black pants suit with white decorations at the neck and sleeves. She asked her, "How do you like it?"

"It's charming," she said. "You look well in it."

Mabel made a face. "And who sees me here? No one. I even rushed to let in the doctor so I'd get a look of male admiration. But he had too big a hangover to even look my way. What did he tell you?"

"He thinks I'm all right again."

"You look fine!" Mabel said, staring at her. "And I liked that gold knit dress you had on the night you were taken ill."

"It's one of my favorites."

"It suits you so well."

She went over to the closet with the idea of looking at it and seeing if she'd soiled it any that night. She opened the door of the closet and looked for the dress, but couldn't see it.

She hesitated and said, "It must be in the other closet."

"Oh?" Mabel looked interested.

She went to the other closet and opened it. Now she reached in quickly and made a frantic search. And with the same result. She turned to Mabel with a shocked expression. " It doesn't seem to be in either closet!"

The lovely blonde girl said, "You didn't check the other closet very carefully. Look in it again."

"I will," she said, and rushing back to the other closet she went through it thoroughly. Then she turned to Mabel once again and said despairingly, "It doesn't make sense! The dress has vanished!"

Chapter Ten

The blonde Mabel was staring at her with a strange light in her large blue eyes. And in an awed voice she said, "I think I know what's happened."

She faced the other girl. "What do you mean?"

"I knew she was in the house last night. I could feel it!" Mabel said tensely.

"Please, explain what you're talking about and what it has to do with my missing dress?" Lucy demanded.

"You shouldn't need it explained," Mabel said.

"Please!" she insisted.

"It was Sheila," Mabel said.

"Sheila?"

"She has come and taken your dress! I told you things appeared and vanished in this house without any explanation. And that is what has happened to your dress."

"Don't ask me to believe a ghost took it!"

"Why not?"

"It makes no sense!"

Mabel's lovely face showed a cynical expression. "It makes as much sense as her ghost placing that pearl pin in your jewel box."

"Charles said he did that."

"To cover up," the other girl said. "He wouldn't want you to know a ghost was at work in the house. He told you that so you wouldn't panic."

"You're saying the phantom put the pearl pin in my jewel box and now has stolen my dress?"

"Yes. I've seen Sheila's ghost, so I happen to believe she returned. And this is the sort of mischief she does."

Lucy stood before the open closet door uncertainly. She knew that she had also seen and heard something since coming to the lodge. And for want of a better explanation it might be termed the phantom presence of the late Sheila. But she could not associate the faint shadowy form with the theft of her dress. That seemed to be taking it too far.

She said, "I don't think any ghost took my dress!"

"Think what you like," Mabel said. "And so will I."

"Perhaps it was soiled and Mrs. Warren

took it to clean," she suggested.

"Never," the pretty blonde wife of Ned said. "She's not the sort to touch anything unless given permission."

"One of the other servants, then?"

"Who?" Mabel demanded in a mocking tone.

And she knew that the possibility of any of the other servants touching the dress was slim indeed. So slim that it wouldn't be worthwhile questioning them.

In a baffled voice she said, "I don't know."

"Sheila returns and wanders through the corridors of the lodge, so why shouldn't she do other things?"

Lucy shook her head. "No!"

"You can protest all you like," Mabel told her. "But in the end you'll find that Sheila's phantom is at the bottom of this. I promise you that."

"And I say you're wrong," she challenged her.

"I wonder," Mabel said significantly, and she wandered away from the room, leaving Lucy there alone. When she was by herself again, Lucy searched through both closets a second time without success.

It was inevitable that she'd go downstairs and seek out Mrs. Warren and ask the prim housekeeper about it. She ended with, "I thought you might have taken it for cleaning."

"No, Mrs. Prentiss," the gray-haired woman with the thick glasses said. "I would never do that without your permission."

"I was ill at the time. I'd worn that outfit the night I became ill."

"Makes no difference, Mrs. Prentiss," the older woman said. "I would never take any of your things without advising you. And you were in your nightgown when I discovered you so ill."

"There's some mystery," she said. "The dress has to be some place in this house."

The prim woman eyed her nervously. "Some odd things have taken place here before, Mrs. Prentiss. I wouldn't press it too far."

Again she was amazed that the woman seemed afraid to discuss the matter. She said, "I know there have been a lot of wild stories, but I don't listen to them."

"I would if I were you," Mrs. Warren advised her. "And I'd wait. The dress will likely turn up."

"It's my very best one," she protested. "And I refuse to have it taken from me without making any effort to get it back!"

"Just as you like Mrs. Prentiss," the

housekeeper said in her prim fashion.

"Please inquire about it from the other servants," she asked.

"I will, Mrs. Prentiss," Mrs. Warren promised, but there seemed little prospect that she'd come up with anything. Her manner was far too resigned. And while Lucy found the whole thing unbelievable, it seemed the others had been conditioned to such unusual happenings.

In her frustration she found herself going up to visit the one person in the house who she felt had some sympathy for her. When she reached the wireless room she was surprised to see that David was missing and the set was turned off. And while she was standing there, he appeared in the doorway on his crutches.

"I thought I heard you in here," he said, swinging himself in expertly. "I was in my bedroom next door."

"So you're using your crutches openly," she observed.

The youthful face so much like her husband's showed a grim smile. "Just between my bedroom and this room. And sometimes I still use the wheelchair."

She gave him a knowing glance. "You travel a lot further than that on your crutches."

He said, "That's our secret. Remember?"

"I do," she said. "May I ask you in confidence if you've been to the upper room lately?"

He maneuvered himself into his wheelchair and then gave her a wary look. "What if I have?"

"Has there been any more work done on the painting?"

"Yes."

"More art work done by your mother's phantom?"

"I say so."

She said, "Something very strange and annoying has happened to me."

"Did someone try to poison you again?"

"Not again. This time I've been gotten at in a different way. My nice gold knit dress has vanished from my room as if it never existed."

"That's too bad," the boy in the wheelchair said.

"I think so."

"Any ideas?"

"I've asked around, and the general opinion seems to be that it was your mother's ghost who took it."

David said, "That's interesting."

"I think it's stupid!"

"But the dress is gone."

"Of course it's gone," she said.

"We've had other things of that sort happen," David told her. "A favorite dress of my mother's was found laid out on her bed as if she were getting ready to wear it."

"Someone trying to deceive you into believing in the ghost," she said. "Anyone could have done that!"

"But with the dress there was a necklace, a lovely jade necklace, ready to be worn with it. Also one of my mother's favorites."

Lucy said, "Whoever knew about the dress would know about that and place it there in the same way."

David's smile was grim. "That could be true, except for one thing."

"What?"

"My mother was buried with the jade necklace on her neck," he said.

A cold chill raced down her spine as she heard this. She was shocked into silence for a moment before she said, "I still maintain that it must have been a hoax of some sort."

"I wish I felt the same way," David said. "I don't. I think my mother's unhappy spirit is roaming about the lodge, and she'll continue on here until she is avenged."

She said, "I'd hoped you might offer me some sympathy and help."

"Sorry," the youth said. "You want me to be honest, don't you?"

"Yes."

"That's what I'm being. I'm sorry about the dress and that you are so unhappy here. If you'll recall, I warned you that you should leave long before you were poisoned."

"I remember."

Wryly he said, "So don't blame me for what happens."

"I won't," she sighed. "One other thing. If John Rhode and I help you, will you go tobogganing with us?"

David said, "I told you before it was crazy to even think about it."

"I believe in not giving up. Have you changed your mind?"

There was a wistful look on the boy's face. Then in a quite different tone he said, "I appreciate what you're trying to do for me. But it's too much!"

"Only you say that!"

"All right," he said wearily. "I'll think about it. Maybe one day I'll take you up on it. But have you any idea how much trouble it would be getting a cripple to the slope and safely on a toboggan?"

"It could be managed," she assured him. "Just name the day."

"I said I'd think about it," was his firm reply. "I can't promise you a thing."

But she left him with the happy feeling that she had at least made some progress in this and that he would soon break down and agree to go on an outdoor expedition. But the matter of her missing dress still remained unexplained.

Nor did a thorough search of the house help in any way. At last every room had been covered but the locked gun room in the cellar — keys for which were held only by Ned — and the mysterious studio in the attic. She knew that David had a key for it, but he was not liable to give it to her. So if she wished to explore the room, she would have to get the other key from her husband. Whether or not Charles would surrender it was a question.

Neither he nor Ned appeared at the lodge for lunch, and so she had no chance to talk with them. But in the midafternoon she received a phone call from John Rhode.

The man in the house next door said, "I thought it easier to check on you this way. How are you?"

"Completely myself again," she said.

"I'm glad of that," he said gravely.

"There is another complication, though," she admitted.

"What sort?"

She glanced around the hall where she had taken the phone call on an extension and said, "Nothing I want to discuss with you on the phone."

"You make me curious."

"Sorry."

"I called to invite you and Charles over to dinner tonight," John Rhode went on. "Do you think he'll come?"

"I'll insist," she said. "I want to talk to you anyway."

"Fine," he said. "Then we'll see you at sevenish."

"We'll be there," she said, feeling sure she could safely promise for Charles.

So it was arranged. She put down the phone with the first feeling of satisfaction she'd known since she'd discovered that her dress was missing. And then an uneasiness took hold of her. She had the same old desire to escape from the house. And she decided that she was well enough for a short stroll around the grounds.

Going upstairs, she dressed warmly and then came down again, ready for her walk. Mabel was standing in the living room and gazed at her in surprise.

"You're not going out, are you?" the blonde asked.

"Yes. I want some fresh air."

Mabel said, "I don't think the doctor would approve."

"I was poisoned," she said, "not ill. I'm over the poison now and I'm no longer all that weak. The air will do me good."

The attractive blonde shrugged. "If you think so, but I predict Charles will be angry when he comes home."

"I'll risk that," she said and went on out.

The air was cold and the sun had vanished, but she kept close to the house. There was no question that she felt the icy weather a bit more because of her bout in recovering from the poison. But she filled her lungs with the good, fresh air and her head felt clearer.

She made her way to the rear of the lodge and walked around the swimming pool. It was filled with ice at the moment and the area around it was bleak and snow-covered, but she imagined it must be pleasant during the warm summer weather. It was something David should take advantage of to strengthen his leg muscles.

At the same time she tried to decide what her attitude ought to be concerning Sheila's ghost. It seemed that she was des-

265

tined to live in the shadow of the dead woman. The entire life at Seven Timbers in various ways revolved around the mystery of Sheila's death and the fear of her returning ghost. Even she had been infected by it!

The missing dress had brought things to a kind of crisis. And when she saw Charles again she intended to talk to him much more frankly than she ever had before. In fact she had made up her mind she was going to challenge him about the locked studio and ask him for the key to it. She could not go on encouraging his obsession concerning the attic room.

He surely believed, just as David did, that his wife's phantom was returning to complete the painting a little at a time. And Lucy resented this. She felt sure there had to be some explanation about the mystery painting, and she was beginning to wonder if David might be the perpetrator of it to torment his father, rather than being a believer as he pretended.

It was easily possible. She had discovered that the crippled youth was sly. And it also appeared that he blamed those living in the lodge for his mother's death. Moreover, Sheila had turned him against his father with her insistence that Charles' neglect had made his shooting injury possible. It was a weird business, and she felt that David might have done something to her dress to carry out his charade that his mother's spirit was still active in the house, when in fact he was responsible for the happenings.

She thought she'd heard him moving awkwardly along the corridor that night of her illness, before the ghost had come into her room. Was it possible that David moved about even better than she knew and that it had been he who'd entered the bedroom?

It was a fascinating possibility and depended a good deal on whether David knew anything about painting. If she discovered that he had skill with a brush, she'd be ready to believe that he was doing the ghost-painting. But to learn this would take some discreet questioning in the right areas.

So absorbed was she in her thoughts about all this that she was slow in discovering that she wasn't alone. Another figure had come up to stand beside her. She glanced up with surprise to see the smiling, arrogant face of pilot Ben Huggard. Like herself, he was bundled up well against the cold winter day.

He said, "We meet again."

"Yes," she managed.

"You're staying close to the lodge today?"

"I am," she said. "It's too cold to remain out long."

He offered her a mocking smile again. "Especially when one has been ill, and I've heard you were very ill."

"It was only a temporary thing," she told him.

"You were lucky."

"I think so," she said.

"Are you getting to like Seven Timbers any better?" he wanted to know.

"I was never so satisfied with it," she replied. She found him obnoxious company and desperately wanted to get away from him.

He smiled at her again. "I think you pretend you like it but you're actually very frightened here."

Her eyes widened. "What would make you say that?"

"Just knowing what has gone on here," Ben Huggard said in his mocking fashion. "And let me warn you. It won't get any better."

"You think not?" she asked a little angrily.

"No!"

She could not help flinging at him, "How can you be so well advised about your employer's affairs?"

The big man smiled nastily. "I know the Prentiss family and their problems a lot better than you might guess."

"Apparently," she said in a cold voice. "I've heard all I care to from you!" With that, she turned and rushed away from him. She heard him laughing as she fled.

In her urgency and humiliation she chose to walk farther away from the lodge and so found herself ascending the hill to the Prentiss family cemetery. She did not want to go there, but at the same time, she did not want to turn back. She hoped that within a few minutes the boorish Ben Huggard might move on. Then she could safely return to the Lodge.

She reached the cemetery and stood studying it for a moment. Then, for no particular reason other than to keep warm, she began crossing among the gravestones until she came to the spot where Sheila's gravestone marked the mound in the snow. And when she reached the black granite marker she suddenly went rigid and stared at the grave!

There wound around the stone, as if by some insane hands, were the torn remnants of her once-lovely dress. The knit gold had been ripped into rags and then wound around the headstone as a kind of macabre decoration. It was a sickening sight and she continued to stare at the bizarre scene with a sinking heart. She knew that someone hated her enough to do this and also to make an attempt on her life. More than one attempt! It was only a lucky accident that she was alive.

The wintry wind brushed hard against her, and she knew she could not remain up there any longer. With a few quick movements she unwound most of the gold knit material that lay around the monument, desecrating it. Then she crumpled it roughly into a large roll in her hands and turned to make her way back to the lodge.

Tears brimmed from her eyes at the thought of the ugly vandalism. And she stumbled as she made her way down the hill to the rear of the lodge. When she reached the frozen pool there was no sign of the belligerent Ben Huggard, and so she went on to the front of the lodge and inside.

Mabel was in the living room talking to Mrs. Warren when she entered. The two turned and saw the remains of her dress in her hands, and they both registered shock.

Mabel was the first to speak, asking, "Where did you get that?"

"In the graveyard," she told them, holding the torn strips of the once lovely dress up for them to see.

Mrs. Warren's mouth gaped open and the prim woman echoed, "In the graveyard!"

"Yes," she said grimly. "Wrapped around Sheila's marker."

"What a horrible business!" Mabel said, her face pale.

"Yes, isn't it," she agreed acidly.

The blonde girl quickly said, "I warned you that you might run into something of this sort."

"Not quite clearly enough," she told her.

Mrs. Warren was still staring at the remains of the dress. She said, "What a pity! It's ruined!"

"Yes, it is," she said grimly.

"Do you want me to take it and get rid of it?" Mrs. Warren asked.

"No," she said. "I intend to keep it and show it to Charles."

"To Charles?" Mabel said with surprise.

"Yes," she said firmly.

"Whatever for?" Mabel asked.

"I want him to see the vandalism," she said. "Maybe then he will believe our enemy is living rather than dead."

"He won't," Mabel promised her.

"Why are you so certain?" she asked.

Mabel gave her a superior smile. "Because of the studio. You can't forget that he goes up there and locks himself in for hours at a time in tribute to Sheila. He believes her a ghostly force here."

Lucy decided to surprise the blonde girl by agreeing with her. She said, "I'm inclined to think you are right."

This clearly took the blonde a little aback. "You are?" she said in surprise, as Mrs. Warren looked on with a confused expression on her thin face.

"I am," she said. "And I'm going to have some questions for Charles about that room."

"What sort of questions?" Mabel wanted to know.

She gave her an icy glance. "That's a matter between myself and my husband."

"Sorry!" Mabel said with a crimson face. "I didn't mean to intrude."

"Better to make it clear," Lucy said. And she marched on past the two women, taking the tatters of her dress with her. When she reached the bedroom she thrust them away in an empty dresser drawer.

Feeling weary, she then lay down for a

nap. And when she woke up it was late and time for her to dress for dinner. She expected Charles almost every moment, as she finished her hair, but he did not come. He was usually home fairly early in the evening and always came up to sit with her for a little before going down to eat.

But tonight there was no sound of his familiar step on the stairs and in the corridor, accompanied by the tap of his cane. So when she was dressed she went down to see what might be keeping him. She found Ned and Mabel standing in front of the fireplace waiting for her.

Ned at once came to her and said, "Charles won't be home until late tonight."

This came as a shock to her, for she'd promised that he'd go to John Rhode's to dinner. In dismay she asked, "Why not?"

"He had to go up to the junction again. There was a breakdown in the machinery there and they asked him to inspect it," Ned said.

"Why does he always have to go?" she asked.

Ned shrugged. "He knows equipment and I don't. I'm sorry. Is there any reason why it should upset you?"

"Yes, there is," she said. "John Rhode

had invited us to dinner and I'd accepted for him."

Ned gave a low whistle. "That is unfortunate."

"Why didn't he phone me?" she asked.

Ned looked embarrassed. "He asked me to before he left. I put it off. Then I thought it would be time enough to tell you when I got here."

"I see," she said bitterly.

Her husband's younger brother said, "Perhaps you can arrange to visit John another night."

She gave him an impatient look. "I want to see him tonight."

The blonde Mabel eyed her over her glass and said, "It can't be so important you can't put it off!"

"Let me be the judge of that!" Lucy shot back.

Ned's face was flaming red. "I'm sorry," he said. "And I'm also shocked about your dress."

"Thanks," she said.

"What are you going to do?" Mabel asked.

"I'm going to see him as I planned," she said sternly. "I'm not going to break the dinner date."

Ned cleared his throat. "May I escort you over?"

"No, thank you," she told him. "I'll be quite all right."

"What about coming home?" Ned asked.

"I'll manage," she said. "I'm sure John will either see me here or have someone else take care of it."

And she left them to get her coat and hat, wanting no more argument about it. She was shaken that Charles should think so little of her that he'd go off on a business errand without giving her any warning.

Ned was in the living room and he went to the front door with her to see her on her way. Again he apologized, saying, "I feel this shambles is due to my stupidity."

She offered him a brisk parting smile. "I think it might be better to say nothing about it."

"I want you to know I feel badly," he promised her. "And I'm also upset about your dress."

She continued on her way with these parting words in her ears. It was beginning to get dark, and the wind was blowing the snow and making it almost as unpleasant as an actual storm. She took the most direct route across the snow-covered lawns, with her head bent as a protection from the icy winds. At last she reached the front door of the Tudor mansion in which John Rhode lived.

An elderly woman, who she assumed was the housekeeper, answered the door and let her in. A moment later a smiling John came to greet her in the vestibule.

"Glad you could come," he said, and then noticing that Charles had not yet appeared, he asked, "Where is your husband?"

"One guess," she said grimly. "They had an equipment breakdown at the junction and he's gone up there to troubleshoot it."

John's face clouded as he took her coat. "That's too bad. I hoped we might have a good talk."

"I know," she said.

He hung her coat up and escorted her into a living room smaller than the one at Seven Timbers but very comfortable, with a blazing brick fireplace and a beamed ceiling. He inquired her wishes in a drink and then went to a small bar in the corner of the room and poured it for her.

When he came back, he said, "Well, better just you than neither of you."

She took the glass from him with a tiny smile. "I hoped you would say that."

He studied her over his drink. "You look much better."

"Thanks."

"I was very worried about you," he went on.

"And I appreciate your concern," she said.

"How did things go today?" he wanted to know.

She stood there with the flames from the fireplace reflecting on her face and making her look especially lovely as she sighed and told him, "Not well."

John Rhode was at once interested. "Tell me about it."

And she did. She finished with the picture of herself coming into the house with the rags of her dress in her hands. She said, "Of course they still insisted it was Sheila's avenging ghost who was responsible."

"I'm not surprised," Sheila's brother said.

"And what do you think?" she asked.

The gaunt face of the young man facing her was especially grim as he said, "I believe that Sheila was murdered and that you were meant to die of that poison the other night."

She said, "I could not get a proper answer from the doctor as to what had poisoned me."

"Nor should you expect any," John Rhode warned her. "I'd say he is a willing dupe of whoever is trying to carry on this series of murders."

"No proper police up here!" she lamented. "It's very difficult."

John nodded. "The State Police responsible for this area have their headquarters in the next village. And in winter they make the drive over only when they have to."

"I can imagine," she said.

"As for considering that murder was done here, their imaginations don't run that way. They're looking for drunken brawls in saloons and traffic infractions. Their minds can't conceive of murder unless it's the result of some drunken fight."

"Who do you see as responsible for the crimes?" she wondered, hoping that he wouldn't name Charles.

His eyes met hers as he said, "I think you know whom I'm mighty suspicious of."

"Go on."

"Charles." He said it quietly.

She frowned. "How do you figure that out?"

"I think his mental state is bad," his former brother-in-law said. "And he's been worried and haggard ever since we found Sheila dead. I think he killed her because he could no longer stand her nagging that

278

he'd crippled David."

Lucy admitted, "I can see the motive as strong enough to push Charles into such a crime. He loves David dearly, though he tries to hide it. But I can't see Charles as strong enough to be the actual killer."

"How can you be sure?"

"I can't. Ned believes he tried to kill himself when he had that fall."

John Rhode smiled grimly. "And landed in the Portland Hospital, where he had the good fortune to meet you."

"Perhaps he no longer considers it good fortune. It may be he wants to be rid of me too, now that he fears I'll learn the truth about him."

"It's possible," John Rhode said.

"If he has done these things, he has to be mad," she went on. "And if he is mad, he is capable of anything. And his behavior doesn't have to conform to any sensible pattern."

"Exactly my own conclusion," John said.

"So where does that leave us?" she asked with a weary smile.

"With your torn dress," the gaunt, handsome John said.

"Yes," she said. "With my torn dress."

"In a way I wish the criminal would turn out to be Charles," he said. "So you mustn't pay too much attention to me. I want him to be the one."

"Really?"

John's eyes were sober as they met hers. He nodded gently. "Yes. You see, that would be my only hope of having any future with you."

"And if I should be killed in all this plotting?"

"I'm trying to make sure that doesn't happen," the man facing her said.

She turned from him and gazed into the fire thoughtfully and said, "The sad fact is I'm still in love with Charles, even though one part of my mind warns me that he may be a mad criminal. It's very strange!"

"I can understand your dilemma," John Rhode said. "For the sake of Sheila as well as for you I want to try and clear up all this mystery. Then you should have no trouble making up your mind about Charles."

"Especially not if he's guilty," she said, turning to John Rhode again. "But nearly everyone at the lodge believes it is the ghost of an avenging Sheila who is our menace."

"You don't think so."

"No. But there are times when I'm not all that certain," she said, looking up at him with a troubled air. "I think I have seen her ghost at least twice. What about you?"

He was hesitant over her question for a moment, then he said quietly, "Yes. I think I have seen her ghost."

Chapter Eleven

Lucy at once asked him, "Where?"

He gave her a solemn look. "On the grounds at Seven Timbers. One night shortly after her death. I often take midnight walks over that way. And on this night I saw a figure standing on the hill by the cemetery."

"I know where it is," she said.

"I was badly startled to see this figure," John Rhode went on. "But in spite of that I went up there."

"And?"

He looked resigned. "It vanished long before I reached it. But I am still of the opinion that it was Sheila I saw."

"Yet you don't think it is her avenging ghost who is responsible for what is going on now?"

"No," he said.

"Can you tell me if David ever had any training in art or showed any ability in that line?" she asked him.

The stern John Rhode considered. "Yes. I believe he has some talent as an artist. Sheila noticed it when he was young and tried to encourage him. He had some lessons, but he tired of them and gave them up."

"But he did actually study art then?"

"Yes."

"Interesting," she said.

John went on. "As a matter of fact his mother attempted to get him to take up his art again after the accident that crippled him. But he wasn't in the mood for it and turned to the wireless set."

"I thought as much," she said.

"What do you mean?" John Rhode asked.

She gave him a meaningful look. "I think that David is at least partly responsible for the belief that his mother's avenging ghost returns to Seven Timbers."

"Why do you say that?" he asked with a scowl.

"Because of a number of things."

"Tell me," he said brusquely.

"I think David knows more about his mother's death than he has ever let on," she said. "In fact I'd say that if she were murdered, he knows who did it."

John Rhode showed incredulity. "If he

knew that, wouldn't he say?"

"I think not."

"Why?"

"He has a strong reason. At least one that seems strong to him. And part of it is this business of the avenging phantom. He has a key to that upper studio, but you mustn't tell anyone."

John showed further surprise. "How do you know?"

"He told me."

"He trusted you with that information?"

"Yes," she said. "Only Charles is supposed to have a key for up there. And he goes up there and locks himself in with Sheila's paintings. Especially the one that the ghost is gradually completing."

The gaunt-faced man stared at her. "And your claim is that David is the one actually doing the painting?"

"Yes. His father doesn't realize David can get around as well as he does. And he has no idea the boy has a key to the attic room."

"It's an interesting theory," John agreed.

"And since David can paint fairly well, he could finish the painting," she said.

"No doubt about that."

"And I have a suspicion he's not even as badly crippled as he has pretended to me," she said. "I wouldn't be too much shocked if I learned that he could walk without his crutches. At least a little distance."

The man standing by the fireplace with her looked astounded. "You're giving me a completely different picture of things," he said.

"I mean to," she told him. "Perhaps if we can gather all the facts we may be able to solve this riddle."

"Hopefully," he said. "But do we have anywhere near all the facts?"

"Probably not. I still say watch David."

"Under the circumstances, I agree," John Rhode said.

"And don't betray what I've told you about him," she warned. "He is very fond of you."

"Good."

"And he likes me for the moment," she said ruefully. "But he was fond of Mabel once, and because he decided she wasn't playing fair with him he turned strongly against her."

"Oh?"

"Yes. He seems to hate her now. And I don't want to find myself in her shoes."

"No. That would be bad," John agreed. "You can count on my discretion."

She said, "If I hadn't felt I could rely on

you I wouldn't have said anything."

He smiled and glanced at the big grandfather clock in the corner of the room. "Time for us to go in to dinner, or my housekeeper will lose patience with us."

They left the shadowed living room for an equally shadowed dining room, with candles on a white-clothed table and an elegant meal served by the old woman who'd let her in.

She congratulated him on the food. "You do very well here," she said.

"Yes," he said with a tired smile. "I have thought of leaving many times, but there is something to this way of life that I like a great deal."

"I'm sure of that."

He frowned. "Sheila's death changed my feelings to a degree. Unless I find a satisfactory answer to what happened to her I do not want to remain on here."

"If you left, would you sell your share in the firm?"

"Likely," he said.

"I imagine Ned Prentiss would be glad to buy you out," she said. "I think he is very ambitious for the firm. He gives a great deal of himself to it."

"More than I would ever care to," the man at the table with her admitted.

"I'm not sure his marriage will last," she added. "So he has the chance of failure there."

"I wonder if he cares," John Rhode said.

"I think so," she said. "I have an idea he is extremely jealous of Mabel. But I also have the feeling she has a lover in Montreal."

"You mentioned that Ben Huggard spoke of that to you."

"Yes," she said. "He was reveling in it. He hates the Prentiss family, so he loved the idea of them being disgraced."

"Ben is far from a likable fellow," John agreed.

"I try to avoid him whenever I can," she said.

"That sounds a wise plan," John Rhode said. "I have an idea he likes to carry tales."

They finished dinner and lingered at the table for a long while. Then they returned to the living room for cordials and more conversation. By the time Lucy decided to leave it was after ten o'clock.

She rose and said, "Perhaps if we phoned Charles he'd be home and he could come over and get me."

Also on his feet, John said, "No. If he is home he'll be dead tired. I'd much prefer to escort you back."

"Very kind of you!" she said.

"My pleasure," he told her. He fetched her coat, then bundled himself up against the cold night, and they started out. There were no moon or stars and the dark night hinted of a possible storm.

As they walked across the expanse of frozen snow he said, "Try to keep a close watch on David."

"I intend to," she said.

"And I'm going to make some inquiries in the village that I meant to make long ago," he said. "It's beyond procrastinating any longer."

"There's no question of that," she agreed.

"I hope Charles won't be angry because you came to dinner with me alone," the man at her side said.

"He oughtn't to be," she said. "I made the engagement in good faith. And because it was so urgent that we should talk I didn't want to put if off any longer."

"Exactly," John said.

"He can be unreasonable," she admitted. "But I hope not in this case."

They reached the entrance of Seven Timbers, and he said goodnight to her at the bottom of the verandah steps. She watched him walk off into the dark night with a distinct feeling of uneasiness. She had been able to relax in his company and feel there was some hope. But now that she was left alone to face Charles and the others in the sinister old lodge she began to feel the old familiar fears.

John vanished into the darkness, and she was about to walk up the steps and go inside when from a distance she heard her name wailed on the wind. It came to her in such an eerie manner that she halted and looked back over her shoulder with a shocked expression on her pretty face.

Then her name was riding on the wind once more! "Lucy! Lucy!" it came in a moaning voice.

She slowly turned and descended the steps to the snow once again, trying to sort out the direction from which her name was being called. And as she listened and tried to detect the area, she moved farther and farther out across the lawn until she was twenty feet or so from the verandah. The wailing stopped, and she was about to turn and go back to the house when something else happened.

Seemingly from out of nowhere there came a roaring sound. And as she turned in horrified surprise to the direction from which it came, she was blinded by a strong headlamp that was bearing down on her at a shocking speed. The thing came directly at her, and she screamed and literally had to hurl herself full length to the right of its path to escape it.

She fell sprawling in the snow face downward as the skidoo roared by and went on until it was over the hill and out of sight. She lay trembling in the snow, not sure yet whether she'd been hit or not. With a tiny moan she raised herself. And then realizing that the vicious rider might decide to make a return journey across the lawn, she struggled to her feet and ran over to the verandah steps.

Gripping the railing she dragged herself up to the verandah, and then went to the door and opened it. As she stumbled inside a distraught Mrs. Warren came toward her.

"Mercy me!" the prim woman exclaimed. "What has happened to you, Mrs. Prentiss?"

She leaned her weight against the thin woman and moaned, "I was out on the lawn and a skidoo came roaring by and tried to deliberately run me down."

"I heard it," the thin woman said. "But I had no idea it was anything more than a nuisance. I didn't know you were out there!"

She allowed the housekeeper to lower

her into an easy chair as she said, "He tried to kill me!"

"Probably didn't even see you," the older woman said with indignation. "You're dressed dark. And they oughtn't to trespass — but they do!"

"It's only luck I'm not dead now," Lucy lamented.

"I'll get you a hot drink," Mrs. Warren said in a motherly fashion. "Did you hurt yourself in the fall?"

"I think not," she said.

"Then a hot drink may be the best thing for you." She glanced up at the gray-haired woman. "Where are the others?"

Mrs. Warren said, "Mr. Charles has not come back yet and Mr. Ned is at the mill. I rather expect Mr. Ned will stay there until Mr. Charles returns from the junction to report to him. Then they will likely both come back here together."

"Yes."

"Mrs. Mabel is upstairs asleep, and I guess young David is still sitting up with his wireless. At this time of night he gets all kinds of distant places like Australia and India. It's a marvel."

"Yes, it is," she said without any real interest as she took off her coat, which was still caked with snow.

"I'll take that and get you the hot drink," Mrs. Warren said as she picked up the coat and started out to the kitchen.

Lucy, left alone, went over and stood before the remains of the log fire in the fireplace. She wondered if John Rhode had heard the skidoo that had almost taken her life. No doubt he had, but he probably hadn't thought anything of it. Unhappily the motorized machines raced across private properties at all hours of the day and night without regard.

The question she was now asking herself was whether this was just an ordinary skidoo rider or someone deliberately wanting to maim or kill her?

Coming on top of everything else it was a new and troubling question. And it served to show her that she was constantly to be in danger. How had her name come to her on the wind in ghostly fashion? Who had been responsible for that? Was it truly the ghost of Sheila that she'd heard?

When Mrs. Warren came back with a tray holding a tall mug of hot Ovaltine, she took it eagerly and drank it. Soon she began to feel the warm liquid spreading through her and giving her some hint of aliveness once again.

Mrs. Warren watched over her anxiously,

"Do you feel better now?"

"Yes," she said. "I was almost in the house and then I heard my name whispered on the wind."

The prim woman looked upset. "Whispered on the wind?"

She glanced up at her. "I heard it clearly. My name being called in a sort of wailing tone. It came over and over again."

"That's very odd, Mrs. Prentiss," the housekeeper said nervously. "I mean, coming after all that has happened with the dress and all."

"I know."

"It has to be the ghost," Mrs. Warren said with an unusual tremor in her voice.

She shook her head. "I don't know. I would have been safely in the house if I hadn't listened to that wailing and gone out to try to locate it."

The gray-haired Mrs. Warren eyed her fearfully from behind her hornrimmed glasses. "She lured you out there!" she said in a taut whisper.

She glanced at the older woman. "Yes, you might say that."

She was finishing the hot drink when the front door opened and Charles came in. She was surprised to see that he was alone. And he seemed just as surprised to find her seated there in a dinner dress at this late hour.

He came across to her. "You're up late!"

"Yes," she said. "Where's Ned?"

He registered surprise on his weary, handsome face. "How should I know? Isn't he at home?"

"No," she said. "According to Mrs. Warren he went back to the mill expecting you to meet him there. He's probably there waiting for you right now."

Charles asked Mrs. Warren, "Is that so?"

The housekeeper said, "Yes, sir." And to Lucy she said, "Will you need me any more?"

"No, thank you," Lucy told her. "It was good of you to go to all this bother for me."

"Not at all, Mrs. Prentiss," the housekeeper said. "It's part of my job. Goodnight." And she took the tray and vanished in the direction of the kitchen.

Meanwhile Charles had put through a call to the mill office on the hall phone. Now he returned and said, "I managed to catch Ned. I told him I came directly here, and he's coming home."

"Good," she said.

He stared at her. "You're up late, but I guess I said that before. And you're dressed very special. What does it mean? You ought to be in bed after your sick spell."

She met his eyes coolly. "After being poisoned, don't you mean?"

"Well, whatever," he said with a resigned air.

She told him, "I had accepted a dinner engagement for us with John Rhode, not knowing you'd been called away."

"Oh?" He seemed surprised.

"When Ned told me you wouldn't be able to make it, I decided to go alone."

Charles showed even more surprise. "You actually went over there to dinner alone?"

"Yes. What harm was there in that?" she challenged him.

He looked a little uneasy. "None, I suppose. I'm sure you could have put the engagement off to another night. Social life here in the village isn't all that hectic."

Her eyes met his in a firm glance. "The point was that I didn't want to put it off. I had some things I wanted to talk to him about. Things important to me."

"I see," he said.

"I could even say, important for us," she went on. "And after we had dinner and a talk he brought me back."

Charles seemed to accept it all in

pleasant enough fashion. He said, "Did you have an enjoyable evening?"

"Yes."

"And were you able to settle any of the points bothering you?" he wanted to know. "I'm sure if he talked about me it wasn't too complimentary. He still blames me for Sheila's death."

"She was his sister and close to him," she said. "I think you should be able to understand that and forgive him for it."

"I hold no enmity as far as he's concerned," Charles said. "But there is a strangeness about him. He's a loner."

"There are worse things."

Charles stood there studying her in the after-midnight shadows of the big living room. He asked, "What did you two discuss?"

"Many things," she said evasively. "What upset me most was something that happened afterwards."

"What?"

She told him about the skidoo and how it almost ran her down. She said, "I'm certain it was a deliberate attack on me."

The handsome face of her husband showed doubt. "But they come riding across the property all the time. It could merely have been a coincidence that you were out there. And you were dressed in dark clothes, it would have been hard to see you."

"But who lured me out there?" she persisted. "Who called out my name? I heard it on the wind."

He hesitated. "I can't answer that. But isn't it true that we sometimes conjure sounds out of the wind that aren't really there?"

"You're saying that hearing my name wailed in the wind was imagination on my part?"

"I'll say it is likely that it was," Charles said. "I don't mean to be argumentative, but that's my opinion."

She said forlornly, "If you think that, then there's no use discussing the rest of it."

"I think you made a mistake going to John Rhode's alone. What happened afterward was merely a result of it. If you hadn't been out there the incident of the skidoo couldn't have taken place."

"Your reasoning is unfair," she protested.

"I'm sorry," he said, looking dreadfully weary. "Let us go up to bed before Ned gets here. He'll want to ask me a lot of questions about the mill breakdown, and I don't feel up to talking about it."

This surprised her a little, but she saw the good sense of it, so she said, "Very well."

They went up the right stairway and down the corridor to their bedroom. When they went inside she crossed to the table and picked up the scraps of her gold knit dress and brought them over to show him.

Standing before him she displayed the torn rags of the once lovely dress and said, "Now tell me this is my imagination!"

He looked astounded and fingered the cloth. "Was this your dress?"

"It was," she said with irony.

"What happened?"

She told him, and when she revealed the way she'd found it tied around the tombstone of his first wife, his face went deathly pale and she could see him trembling a little.

He held the remnants of the dress in his hands and told her, "I'll see that whoever is responsible will pay for this."

She gave him a questioning look. And she asked calmly, "And how do you propose to go about it?"

He didn't reply at once, but he gave her a haunted look as he said, "I don't just know."

"Everyone seems to believe that Sheila's ghost is responsible for this mischief."

Charles let his mouth gape open. "You surely don't listen to that kind of nonsense?"

She said, "The evidence is piling up. I'm not so sure the possibility of Sheila's ghost haunting the lodge is all that unlikely."

Charles raised a protesting hand. "Please!"

"You brought me into this without any warning," she said. "Had I known all the facts I might not have married you."

"Lucy!" he said in a pleading tone.

"I fell in love with you," she went on. "And so I'm here now. But I need some help from you. I want evidence of your faith in me."

"Have I ever denied that?"

She said, "I think so. But we won't argue about the past. I'll ask you to offer me convincing proof now that I come first in your life."

"Anything," he said.

Her eyes met his. "Give me the key to the attic room."

"The attic room?" he repeated uneasily.

"You know," she said. "I want the key to Sheila's studio."

"Why?" he said with a harried look, as if

he realized she'd managed to trap him.

"I want to see what the attraction is for you up there."

"Anything but that," he protested.

"You made no limitations before," she said evenly. "Why is the room so important to you? Why have you at times gone up there and locked yourself in?"

"You wouldn't understand!"

"Try me."

He hesitated again, with a look of anguish on his handsome face. "It has nothing to do with you! The room has a sentimental meaning for me because of Sheila. Her paintings — are up there."

She said, "What is so special about that? Her paintings are hanging all over the house."

Charles looked continually more uneasy. "The paintings up there are her last ones," he said. "The ones she did just before her death."

"So?"

"One of them is unfinished," he went on unhappily. "I often go up there and sit wondering what was on her mind those last days and hours before her death."

"Do you think that fair to me?" she demanded.

He turned away, his back to her, and

waved a hand out despairingly. "It has nothing to do with you!"

"So you say, but I think it has," she told him. "And that is why I ask you for that key!"

He swung around to face her again with a troubled gleam in his eyes. "What good will it do you to have the key?"

"I'll be able to see the room for myself."

"There's nothing to see."

"Will you allow me to decide that?" she asked. "Haven't I gone through enough? You've seen the torn dress, you know the other things that have happened."

"Having the key to that room won't stop them from happening," he warned.

"Maybe or maybe not," she said. "Anyway I'd like to find out. And I'd like you to stop going to the room. So give me the key."

"Suppose I refuse to?" he asked.

"Then I will have to believe our marriage has been a mistake," was her calm reply. "That we have finally come to a breaking point in it."

He gazed at her in despairing silence for a few moments. Then he said, "You insist on the studio key?"

"Yes!" She somehow knew this was a moment of crisis. That she must not give in at all.

"All right," he said, a strange, grim look on his handsome face. He reached in his pocket and from a keyring disengaged a long, slender key. "There it is," he said, handing it over to her.

"Thank you," she said.

"What are you going to do with it?"

"I'll decide that," she told him.

"In other words, this has become a test of wills on your part?" he suggested.

"Call it that if you like," she told him as she clenched the key in her hand.

"There is nothing up there for you."

"I know."

Charles said, "I'm sorry I've let things go so far. I will find out about that dress."

"We'll see," she said. "In the meantime I'll have this key."

He looked at her in distress. "Please don't disturb anything up there!"

"I won't," she promised.

"You don't understand," he went on in a tortured way. "You don't understand at all."

"I only ask your faith in me," she said.

"You have that," he told her, "I swear it!"

And as if to prove it he took her in his arms and kissed her several times. Even this show of emotion did not completely

302

convince her. She had a fear that he was offering it to placate her rather than as a result of his love for her. He had given her the key to the room with reluctance, and he had said nothing about the ghost painting — though she knew he must indeed have been referring to it when he'd asked her promise that she not disturb anything. But even as she regretted that she could not have complete trust in him, she could also find encouragement in having the key. He had given it to her, even though he'd done so reluctantly. He had made that much progress.

When he released her, he gazed down into her face with a plaintive expression and in a taut voice asked, "Are you in love with John Rhode? Is that why you went over there tonight?"

"No!" she protested. "You should know better than that."

He stared at her. "You do like him?"

"Of course I like him. I think he is my friend. Our friend," she said.

Charles shook his head. "Never my friend!" And he left her and began preparing for bed.

Little was said between them. When Charles was ready to put out the light, he came to her again and kissed her in bed.

She smiled up at him.

He said, "I'm sorry we argued so much. And I am worried about all that happened to you."

"I know you are," she said.

He hesitated above her bed a moment longer, then said an awkward goodnight. After which he put out the light, and she heard him get into bed.

Then came the long wait for sleep. The horror of her narrow escape from the mysterious skidoo rider still took its toll from her. And going over the business of the dress again had not made things any easier. She knew that Charles resented her seeing John Rhode alone, but she also knew that most of her hope of saving her marriage, and perhaps her life, rested in the help that the stern brother of Sheila was offering her.

As usual the night winds had come up again. And she recalled hearing her name on the wind and being lured from the verandah. It had been a weird effect, but it could have been managed easily by a human hiding somewhere. Charles, as usual, preferred to think it had been a product of her overwrought nerves. But she knew better!

The old lodge creaked and groaned in

the wind! What a place it was for ghosts, here in this remote, snow-laden wilderness. Even the people living here had taken on a cold, contained manner that must in part come from their environment. And Charles seemed to be haunted by more than normal fears.

Did he have some guilty secret concerning Sheila's death? And was the bitter, crippled David a party to it? Was that why he kept himself shut up in that tiny wireless room? Why his whole personality had changed from the moment of his mother's mysterious death?

Was it possible that she'd stepped into the shoes of a murdered woman? And was she meant to die in some similar way? She could have died if that skidoo had struck her, and it would most likely have been put down as an accident. Regrettable, but an accident.

Now in the other bed Charles began to talk in his sleep again. She raised herself up on an elbow and stared into the darkness and listened. She was almost afraid she might hear his words too plainly. Afraid that they might tell her more than she wanted to know. For despite all her doubts and suspicions, she did not want to discover that the handsome husband she'd come to love was a murderer!

Charles tossed in his bed and murkily, through clenched teeth, murmured, "Sheila!" And then, "The room! Must not go! The painting!" Then he was silent again.

She thought that perhaps he'd finished, but without any warning he once again began to ramble. His words were blurred at the start, but then he clearly said, "The ghost! Her ghost! It must be there! Must be!" And he trailed off into a lot of incoherent mumbling again.

This proved to be the end of it. But it had effectively decided her against attempting sleep. She quietly got out of bed and put on her dressing gown. Then she took the key, which she'd placed under her pillow, and put it in the pocket of the gown. The room was almost completely dark, so she had to grope her way to the door and open it with great care. She halted at the door once to be sure that Charles was still asleep. He was.

Once out in the semidarkness of the corridor she moved more swiftly. Reaching the door to the studio stairway, she unlocked and opened it. Then, with her heart beating wildly, she gazed up the stairs with frightened eyes. Something told her that if she went up there at this hour she would make a discovery that perhaps would end all her torment and doubts. And so she proceeded up the stairs.

Reaching the threshold of the haunted room, she felt a cold blast of air in her face. It was like a visitation of the cold phantom presence. She hesitated, her nerves on edge, debating whether it was all foolhardy! Whether she shouldn't turn her back on the unknown that waited for her in that dark studio.

Chapter Twelve

She must not allow her fears to conquer her! She decided that, even though she knew that in the darkness ahead of her there might lie some macabre experience that would leave her mind twisted and broken forever. She had to take the risk! So with trembling fingers she groped for the light switch.

Finding it, she snapped on the overhead light, which was concentrated over the easel. The big white room looked much the same as it had on the last occasion of her venturing there. Apprehensively she crossed the rough planks of the floor and stood before the unfinished landscape. And even to her untutored eyes it was apparent that more of the painting had been completed since the night when she'd first seen it.

The brush was there on the shelf of the easel, and so was the palette of paints. But the painting was still not finished. Whether the hand that was working on it was a living one or one reaching up from the grave, the work was being done slowly. Yet it was all of a piece. The style throughout the painting was the same, and this suggested that the same person had done it all. Sheila? Who could say.

The attic studio was cold, and she pressed her hands about her arms, hugging them to her for warmth. The wind was even more eerie at this high place in the old lodge. And she could understand that with the seeming miracle of the ghost painting, her husband could come to the conclusion that his first wife's ghost was making regular appearances at the easel.

She was about to turn away from the easel and examine some of the paintings stacked against the walls when she heard the sound of a floorboard creaking behind her, and she knew at once that she was no longer alone in the room!

Her blood froze in her veins! She stood there unable to move or cry out! Waiting for the next sound! Wary of attack! It came swiftly enough, and mercilessly as well. Something blunt and hard descended on the back of her head, and she sank into a dark unconsciousness as she slumped to the plank floor.

"Lucy!" the voice was frightened and

youthful and it came through the pain and blackness.

She slowly opened her eyes and saw the white, anxious face of young David. The youth was bent over her as she still lay on the floor.

She murmured, "You."

"I thought you were dead!" he confessed. "I couldn't make you speak!"

"When did you get here?" she asked weakly.

"Just a few minutes ago," he told her. "I knew something was going on. The door was unlocked and the lights were on. Then I saw you on the floor."

She raised herself a little, "You didn't see anyone or anything else?"

He stared at her with boyish dismay. "No. Why?"

She gave a tiny moan. "I was attacked. I was standing by the easel, studying the painting. Someone came up behind me and struck me."

"It wasn't me"

"I know that."

"You didn't see who it was?"

"No," she said.

David gave her a strange look. "Perhaps it was my mother's ghost. She couldn't afford to have you see her."

"You really believe in her ghost," she said worriedly.

"You know that," he said.

"Why?"

"I have to," David told her gravely. "It is my only comfort. I know she will have her way."

"You terrify me when you talk like that," she said, and she struggled to her feet. Her head was aching, and when she touched it she could feel a small lump as a souvenir of the blow.

David worked himself up on his crutches and stared at her with troubled eyes. "Were you hurt badly?"

"I don't think so," she said. "I can only be thankful you came along, or it's hard to say what might have happened to me."

Now he asked accusingly, "How did you get up here?"

"I have a key."

He showed surprise. "Where did you get it?"

"Your father gave it to me."

"I don't believe it!" he gasped.

"He did."

"I can't imagine him doing that. Are you sure you didn't steal it from him?" the youth asked.

"No. I asked for it and I suggested I

would leave Seven Timbers if he didn't give it to me."

"So that's how you handled it."

"Can you think of a better way?"

"I suppose not," David said bitterly. "That's the way women twist men. Mabel uses the same technique on Ned."

She said, "I hope there's a difference. I was doing this for your father's good."

"How do you figure that?"

"I wanted to try to break the spell this room has for him," she told the youth on the crutches.

He shook his head. "You're not likely to do that."

"At least it was worth trying."

He shifted on his crutches and gave her a grim smile. "It didn't get you far."

"It seems not."

"Does he know you're up here?"

"No. He's asleep," she said.

"He'll be angry if he finds out."

"I kept your secret," she said. "You better keep mine. I'll depend on you not to tell him."

David's expression gave no hint as to how he felt about this. He finally said, "I'll see. You could have asked me if you wanted to come here. I would have let you have my key."

She shook her head. "I don't think so."

"I would have!" he insisted.

"You say that now because you know I have a key," she told him. "And what are you doing up here?"

"I like to visit the room and see the painting progress," he said. "And I can only do it when I'm sure no one will see me. It has to be late at night."

"I'm glad you came along."

"Now you'd better leave," he suggested. "Leave while I'm still here. I'll come with you and see you safely to your room."

She smiled wryly. "After what has happened, that is an offer I can't refuse."

Before David left the room he swung himself over to the easel on his crutches and studied the painting with admiration shining on his young face.

Turning to her, he said, "The painting is going to be fine when it's done."

"It is good," she said.

"Mother has a great talent," he said, speaking about her as if she were alive. Then with a sigh he swung back across the room to Lucy, and they both went to the door. He switched off the light and they began descending the stairs.

He saw her to her door and gave her a

whispered goodnight. She went in quietly and saw that Charles was deep asleep. Her head still aching and not much better off for her excursion to the attic studio, she got into bed. She wondered about David, whether he might have struck her down and then perhaps become panicky that he'd killed her. But she decided finally that it hadn't been the crippled youth but someone else who had managed somehow to get away when he or she heard David coming. His slow progress on the crutches and the warning sound they made as he swung along would have given the attacker ample time.

Realizing that the possession of the key and her show of courage hadn't really helped at all, she sank into a troubled, depressed sleep. She did not open her eyes again until the next morning. There was no sun coming in the windows. It was a gray day and it was snowing hard. She was amazed at the frequency with which it snowed in this north country and also at the depth that the continuing falls of snow mounted to.

Charles had left the room, so she got up and quickly washed and dressed. When she went downstairs she found Mabel at the breakfast table.

As she sat down to join her, the blonde girl said with disgust, "I was going to Montreal today but I won't be able to because of the storm."

"Ben Huggard won't fly when it's snowing this hard?" she said.

Mabel grimaced. "He would, but Ned won't let him. I think it's the company plane Ned is worried about, not me."

She gave the other a look of rebuke across the table. "I think you're being unfair to Ned. And didn't you have a trip to Montreal only a little while ago?"

"I need to go again," Mabel said with disgust. "I can't stand it here. Why did you ever marry Charles and come up here?"

"I would expect for the same reason you married Ned. I happened to fall in love with him."

"Ned promised me he'd sell his share of the mill and move to the city," she said with annoyance. "Of course he didn't have any intention of doing it."

"He may have had. But he loves it here," she said. "And that is why he has stayed on hoping you might also get to like it."

"I never will," the pretty blonde said emphatically.

"You were born here and lived here a

large part of your life," Lucy reminded her.

"And I hated it. I hated the house and my family and I got out of here as soon as I could. It was Ned who brought me back with an offer of a job and the promise he'd leave when we were married. So I came back here and worked awhile. Then when we were married he kept finding excuses for not leaving."

"Do you ever visit your family?" she asked.

Mabel's pretty face showed a look of scorn. She said, "My mother is dead and my father is one of the village drunks. Most of my brothers have moved away from here. My father lives with my sister, who is a drudge for her no-good lumberman husband and their five children! Why would I want to visit them?"

"You make a strong case against it," she admitted with a rueful smile. "But they are your family."

"Not anymore, they're nothing to me," the blonde beauty told her. And then abruptly changing the subject, she added, "I hear you were almost run down by a skidoo last night."

She nodded over her coffee cup. "Yes. That's true."

"They drive those things like crazy,"

Mabel said. "It must have been some drunk."

"Perhaps."

"Who else?"

"I haven't decided that yet," she said.

Mabel told her, "I heard Charles and Ned talking about it at breakfast. Charles says he's getting in touch with the state police about it. I've never seen him more upset."

"That's comforting!"

"Not that the state police will find out anything," Mabel went on. "They never do."

The blonde girl left her to finish her coffee alone. When she left the table she crossed over from the dining room to the living room and stood staring out the window at the heavy snowfall. She was watching the great flakes come steadily down when she saw the lights of a car in the snow coming toward the entrance of the house. A moment later she was able to make out the shape of John Rhode's Jeep. She at once went to open the door and let him in.

He got out of the Jeep and came quickly up the verandah steps and over to the door. He stamped the snow off his feet as he said, "Bad morning!"

"Do come in," she urged him.

"Thanks," he said, removing his fur cap. He stepped inside, and she closed the door against the storm. "I've just come from the mill," he explained.

Her eyes widened. "Then you've seen Charles?"

"Yes," the gaunt-faced John said. "I talked with him a short time ago. Just after he arrived at the office."

"Oh?" she said. "I hope he wasn't in a nasty mood."

"I've seen him in better," John Rhode admitted. "But I can't blame him for being upset after what I've heard. He told me about the skidoo that tried to run you down."

"That was after you left me," she said.

"You should have gone straight inside."

"I would have," she said; "but I was sure I heard my name being called."

John Rhode looked grim. "You still should have taken the safe way."

"I know that now."

"I hope so," he said. "I'm going back to the village to see someone, and later in the day I may have something to tell you. Something that will explain a lot of what's been happening."

"Really?"

"Yes," he said. "That's why I came by here now. I wanted to let you know. And to tell you to be careful even when you're inside the lodge."

"I will."

"You remember that," John said, looking at her with grave eyes. "I don't want you to follow in Sheila's footsteps."

"Nor do I want to," she said.

"Then be careful," he warned her again. "Now I'd better be on my way. It's hard to drive in this storm."

"Is it safe to drive?" she wondered.

"No," he said with a wry grin. "But I have no choice if I want to get around."

She saw him out and watched the Jeep disappear into the driving snowstorm. She wondered what the austere John was up to. She was sure that he had hit on something important. He wasn't the sort to rush off on wildgoose chases. After a few minutes more by the window she decided it was time to go up and see David.

She mounted the stairs and went to his wireless room. He had the wireless off and was working at what looked to be a log book. He glanced up from it to give her an interested eye.

"How is your head this morning?"

She smiled wanly. "No worse than if I

had a bad hangover."

"That's bad enough. You worry me," the youth said.

"I'm glad," she told him with a twinkle in her eyes. "That means you still like me."

"Of course I like you," he groaned. "But you always want to poke your nose into trouble."

"I've a naturally curious streak," she said.

"Going up to that room in the small hours is a good example," he said. "Keep that up and something unpleasant is bound to happen to you!"

"I'd resent that if I didn't know you better," she told him.

He said, "Last night ought to have taught you a lesson."

"So everyone says."

"And I don't think it did."

She said, "There are certain things I want to find out, and until I find them out I can't change my ways."

"That means nothing but trouble," the young man at the desk of the wireless room warned her.

"I know," she sighed. "I ought to find myself a different interest, like Mabel. She was all ready to go to Montreal again, but the storm stopped her."

"No one but an idiot would take a private plane out today," David said with youthful disgust.

"She wanted to go. She must have an interesting boyfriend in Montreal."

"No question of that," David frowned. "I feel sorry for Ned."

"He doesn't seem to suspect her."

"I'll bet he does," David said. "Only he's too proud to let on."

"If that's so, Mabel had better be careful. When someone like that finally does go into action, it often ends in murder."

"I think Mabel is too stupid to realize that," David said earnestly. "And by the time she does realize, it will likely be all over for her."

She stared at him. "You think it will break soon?"

"Has to!" David registered disgust. "Ned isn't a complete fool!"

It was at this moment that Mrs. Warren appeared in the doorway of the room, making Lucy worry if the prim woman might have overheard them. The gray-haired woman said, "May I have a word with you, Mrs. Prentiss?"

"Of course," she said. And she turned to David. "I'll see you later."

"Do that," the young man in the wheel-

321

chair said, seeming suddenly uneasy. She guessed it was because he was also thinking that the housekeeper might have listened in on their discussion of the blonde Mabel.

She left him and went out to the corridor to join a waiting Mrs. Warren. The prim woman gave an uneasy glance in the direction of David's room and said, "I think we'd better go on downstairs so we can talk in privacy."

"Very well," she said.

They went down the left stairway to a spot near the fireplace, and here Mrs. Warren stopped and turned to her with a gleam of near desperation showing from behind her thick glasses. She said, "I had to talk to you, Mrs. Prentiss."

"Please do go on!" she begged her.

"Yes, madam," the housekeeper said. "When you spoke of being run down by that skidoo last night, I kind of remembered something. Then I looked for something to refresh my memory, and I recalled some facts I knew that ought to be helpful for you."

"Tell me," she said eagerly.

"It has to do with Mr. Ned," the housekeeper said soberly. "You know about his gun room in the cellar."

322

"Yes. We went by it the day you showed me through the house," Lucy said. "It was locked up then."

"It's always kept locked except for special occasions," Mrs. Warren agreed.

Lucy asked her, "What about the gun room?"

The housekeeper gave a frightened glance around her and then leaned toward her confidentially and said, "There is something to be found out down there."

"Really?"

"Yes, madam," the nervous Mrs. Warren went on. "I didn't intend to tell you. But what happened last night changed my mind. I know who was on that skidoo."

She was alert now. "You do?"

"Yes," the prim Mrs. Warren said in a conspiratorial tone. "I can only go along with being silent so long. Then I have to tell the truth."

"What truth?" she asked.

"I'll let you find out for yourself," Mrs. Warren said. "And you mustn't whisper a word about it to anyone but Mr. Charles. Then whatever he decides will be all right."

"I don't understand," she said.

Mrs. Warren produced a key from her apron pocket and gave it to her. "You will," she said. "Go down to the gun room and you'll see what I've been trying to tell you. And I'll be down there to join you just as soon as I can."

She took the key. "Why don't you come with me now?"

"I have something to make sure of first," Mrs. Warren said in her prim way. "There are things going on in this house you don't know anything about. Things you can't guess!"

"So it would appear," she said, thoroughly excited.

"Some say the ghost of Mrs. Sheila shows herself here," the housekeeper said. "And when you go in that gun room you'll understand something about it."

The housekeeper gave her a sign to be silent and go on her way. She left her and found the door leading to the cellar stairs. It was a great bit of luck to have this unexpected help from Mrs. Warren. She had no idea what surprise waited for her in the gun room. But she realized it would be an ideal spot to hide anyone or anything — this room away from the rest of the house and always kept locked.

It had been her understanding that Ned held the only keys to the place himself. But now it appeared that Mrs. Warren also had a key. And so she was going to be able to explore the room for herself with the housekeeper's key and find out what secret it held.

The cellar was in darkness except for the scattered, tiny bulbs that glowed an indifferent yellow from high in the shadows of the ceiling. She slowly made her way along the earthen floor of the cellar toward the door to the gun room. It occurred to her that this had to be the ideal place for a ghost. It was always night down here, and so Sheila's ghost might always enjoy a refuge in the darkness.

The thought of Sheila's ghost sent an icy shiver through her. After last night she knew she must be wary. John Rhode had warned her to be cautious even in the lodge. She wasn't being too cautious now, venturing alone into this phantom darkness, but she had to take some risks if she were to learn the truth about all that had gone on.

Now she was at the door of the gun room. Nervously she fitted the key in the lock. It worked and she opened the door. It was black inside, and she groped a hand in to find a wall switch. When she turned it on, the big room, with its walls lined with guns, was revealed. The neat racks held weapons of every sort, guns large and small. And the shelf that ran around the room also held weapons, in the process of being repaired, and parts for their repair. It was a fascinating place.

She slowly stepped inside, not knowing what she might see and expecting to find almost anything. The thing that caught her attention at once was a door. It struck her that what she was searching for must be hidden behind that door. The phantom figure that had been so elusive and that had threatened her more than once had to be there!

Nerves on edge, she started across to the door. And then it struck her that she should have a weapon. And she was in a room filled with them. Not that she could expect all of them to be loaded for use, but any one of the rifles could serve as a kind of makeshift club if necessary. She quickly snatched a huge rifle from the shelf and balanced it so that she could swing it if she had to. Then she stealthily began her advance to the door again.

When she reached it she thrust out a hand and gently touched the knob. She was too tense to breathe as she gently turned the knob to open the door. But the knob resisted her. The door was locked!

Then from behind her there came the sound of someone entering the room. Turning, she saw that it was Mrs. Warren. And she gave a cry of welcome to the prim woman. "I'm so glad you're here!"

"Yes, I know," Mrs. Warren said dryly, fixing a strange stare at her from behind those thick glasses.

She then noticed that the prim housekeeper was wearing black gloves and that she carried one of Ned's ancient guns in her hand. She said, "You armed yourself too. I found this gun. It isn't loaded but it makes a sort of weapon."

"This is loaded," the prim woman said crisply, taking a few steps toward her.

"Good," she said. "But the door is locked. And I suppose the secret, whatever it is, lies behind that door."

The gray-haired housekeeper shook her head. "No," she said softly, "the secret lies within me."

Puzzled by her talk and actions and the strange look in her eyes, Lucy ventured, "What do you mean?"

"You're going to die," the woman said harshly. "You stole the key to this room from my keyring in the office and came here. You found this gun I have in my hand and you held it carelessly and it went off!

You were curious and stupid and you killed yourself!"

She stared at the woman, who'd taken another step toward her. "Like Sheila!" she said.

The prim Mrs. Warren nodded, "Like Sheila!"

"Why?"

"No time," the prim woman said, holding the gun at a certain angle. "Don't try to move! It will only make it more messy!"

"Please!" she begged, and balanced the gun as she prepared to use it as a club against the obviously mad housekeeper.

"Don't lift that gun!" Mrs. Warren shouted, taking aim with her own weapon.

But she did not fire it as she'd hoped. For at that instant a figure who'd been crouching in the shadows came forward with a giant leap and grasped her around the arms. There was a struggle and Mrs. Warren screamed. Then as the frantic struggle continued, Lucy pressed close against the door, completely terrified, knowing that the gun could go off wildly at any moment and kill any of them!

The struggle was not a long one. It ended with the gun firing, as Lucy had anticipated, and with the prim Mrs. Warren falling back with a shrill scream. She stared at them wild-eyed as the gun dropped from her hand and a growing patch of red spread across her neat white apron. Then she fell to the floor of the gun room.

A disheveled David stood over the fallen woman, breathing heavily from his exertions. He turned to look at Lucy with a grim expression on his young face.

And at that moment all she could think of to say was, "You can walk!"

"I've been walking for months," he said with disgust. "But I didn't intend anyone should find out!"

She stepped over to the fallen woman, who was stretched out on her back with her eyes still staring wildly at the ceiling. She said, "We'd better find out if she's alive."

"I hope she isn't," David said bitterly.

Lucy knelt by the old woman and tried to locate some vital signs. There were none. She looked up at David and in an awed voice said, "She's dead."

"Better her than us," was his reply.

But the melee wasn't to end at that. For it was then that Mabel chose to appear in the doorway of the room. She took a single look at the dead woman in the pool of blood on the floor and turned and ran off screaming.

Lucy felt she might faint. She said, "Someone ought to go and try to calm her."

"Not me!" David said.

"And we have to let Charles know," she said. "We have to tell your father what has happened and have him come here at once."

David looked a little less sullen. He said, "I'll phone him and you can look after Mabel."

With that he surprised her by walking out of the room in a remarkably steady fashion. She remained by the corpse of the housekeeper a moment longer and then went to find Mabel.

She searched the house, but there was no sign of the blonde girl and her coat was gone. She came down to the living room, where David was slouched in an easy chair, and went across to him.

"I can't find her," she said. "She's gone! She's not in the house!"

David smiled grimly. "I didn't expect her to be. She was in on it, you know."

"What?" she said incredulously.

"Wait until my father gets here," was all the satisfaction the youth would give her.

Charles arrived about five minutes later, and Ned and John Rhode were with him.

Charles crossed to her at once and asked, "What about Mrs. Warren? Is she really dead?"

She nodded. "In the gun room." Both Charles and Ned hurried by her, while John Rhode remained to stand, between her and the chair where David was sitting.

John Rhode took off his snow-laden coat and said, "I told you to be cautious, and you weren't."

"How did you know?" she asked.

"A long story," John said. And he turned to David and said, "I think you might as well begin it by telling us who killed your mother."

David's youthful face was solemn. "Mrs. Warren killed her. She shoved her down the stairs after mother and Mabel had a big fight. Mother had found out that Mabel was sleeping with Ben Huggard, and she promised she was going to tell Ned. Then Mrs. Warren came out of the shadows and attacked my mother and killed her. Mabel didn't do anything but scream like a ninny, the way she did today. I was hiding in the shadows of the corridor and saw it all."

She said, "You knew this all along?"

"Sure," he said defiantly. "I waited there hoping my mother wouldn't be dead. But

331

when I heard Mrs. Warren tell Mabel that she'd broken her neck, I knew there was no hope. And I heard Mrs. Warren quiet Mabel down and take her away."

"Why?" she demanded.

"I found that out only this morning," John Rhode said. "From Mabel's drunken father. Only he isn't her father, but her adopted father. His wife wasn't Mabel's mother. Mabel was Mrs. Warren's daughter, born out of wedlock and brought up by this friend and her husband. Mrs. Warren had her pretend the child was hers. And only when the woman died did she reveal the truth to Mabel."

"How did they manage it?" Lucy asked.

"Easily. The family were living in a tiny village a good distance from here. Mrs. Warren stayed with them until her baby was born. No one in Seven Timbers knew the child didn't belong to the other two. She was a year or so old when they moved here."

David spoke up, "I made up my mind I'd avenge my mother. But I had to wait until the right time. Then you came along, and Mrs. Warren tried to upset you and the rest of us by pretending my mother's ghost was returning."

Lucy said, "So she was Sheila's ghost."

John Rhode said, "Without a question. And I am sure she had a key to that attic room and sent Mabel up there every so often to fill in the phantom painting. Mabel had taken lessons from Sheila."

David said, "What a corny idea!"

"Not all that corny," John told him. "It fooled your father. Then apparently Mrs. Warren felt that it was only a matter of time until Lucy here found out the truth about Mabel. And since her one aim was to protect her foolish daughter and see she didn't lose her wealthy husband, she planned that Lucy should die in an accident like poor Sheila."

Lucy said, "And the man on the skidoo was?"

"Ben Huggard, without a doubt. He couldn't afford to be exposed either."

Lucy said, "She must have run off to meet Ben now."

John nodded gloomily. "My bet is, snowstorm or no snowstorm, those two are on their way out of the village now. They've likely gone off in Ben's station wagon."

"Good riddance," David said.

His father and Ned appeared, both men looking pale and shocked from what they'd seen. Charles looked at his son accusingly, "All this time you've been able to walk, and you let me suffer on thinking you were crippled."

David remained in the chair. "I don't walk all that well yet. And I had to do it for Mother."

John Rhode gave Charles a significant glance. "You see someone remained loyal to Sheila."

Charles crimsoned. "Are you suggesting that I didn't?"

"No," his former brother-in-law said. "I'm only suggesting that David did it better." He picked up his coat and turned to Lucy. "I'll be going now. It's all over. And it seems that there's no need for me any longer."

She gave him a grateful look. "You've been so kind. I'll see you again."

"Often," he said with a smile. And he told Charles, "You know the police should be sent for as soon as possible."

"I'll look after it," Charles promised.

Ned, looking white and ill, came forward and said, "No. Let me do it. I'll call from the mill. I'm going to the village to see about Mabel and Ben. I expect they've gone, but I want to make sure."

He and John left at the same time, though they took different routes in the still heavy snowstorm. David raised himself out of the chair and moved to the stairway.

He said, "When the police come I'll be in the wireless room." And with that he walked upstairs and vanished down the hall.

Charles glanced after him with a look of wonder on his weary, handsome face. Then he turned to her. "A miracle!"

She said, "A day of miracles. The shadow is lifted!"

He frowned. "There are a lot of things I still don't understand."

"We have plenty of time for that before the police arrive," she said. "Right now I want you to take me in your arms, kiss me, and tell me it will be all right."

And he did.

We hope you have enjoyed this Large Print book. Other Thorndike, Wheeler or Chivers Press Large Print books are available at your library or directly from the publishers.

For more information about current and up-coming titles, please call or write, without obligation, to:

Publisher
Thorndike Press
295 Kennedy Memorial Drive
Waterville, ME   04901
Tel. (800) 223-1244

Or visit our Web site at:
www.gale.com/thorndike
www.gale.com/wheeler

OR

Chivers Large Print
published by BBC Audiobooks Ltd
St James House, The Square
Lower Bristol Road
Bath BA2 3SB
England
Tel. +44(0) 800 136919
email: bbcaudiobooks@bbc.co.uk
www.bbcaudiobooks.co.uk

All our Large Print titles are designed for easy reading, and all our books are made to last.